The House at World's End

Monica Dickens, the great-grand-daughter of Charles Dickens, lives with her husband and two children in America, surrounded by horses, cats and dogs. Author of the famous *One Pair of Hands* and *One Pair of Feet*, autobiographies of her early life, she has written such successful novels as *Kate and Emma* and is also the author of *Follyfoot*, *Dora at Follyfoot* and *The Horses of Follyfoot*, bestsellers published in Piccolo.

Also published in Piccolo are her other books in the World's End series: *Summer at World's End*, *World's End in Winter* and *Spring Comes to World's End*.

Monica Dickens

The House at World's End

Cover and text illustrations
by Peter Charles

Piccolo
Pan Books in association with Heinemann

First published 1970 by William Heinemann Ltd
This edition published 1972 by Pan Books Ltd,
Cavaye Place, London SW10 9PG,
in association with William Heinemann Ltd
3rd printing 1978
© Monica Dickens 1970
ISBN 0 330 02955 X
Printed and bound in England by
Cox & Wyman Ltd, London, Reading and Fakenham

AUTHOR'S NOTE

The lines of poetry quoted in the book are from the following poems:

'I think I could turn and live with animals'
— from *Song of Myself* by Walt Whitman

' "Is there anybody there?" said the traveller'
— from *The Listeners* by Walter de la Mare

'Strong gongs groaning as the guns boom far,
Don John of Austria'
— from *Lepanto* by G. K. Chesterton

One

'There's a cat in your bed!'

'No, no – how could there be? No, Aunt Val, please!'
Carrie tried to hold the kitten quiet with her toes, but when
Aunt Valentina thumped her fat hand on the covers, the
kitten pounced. A tiny curved claw stuck up through the
blanket, and Aunt Val pulled back her hand with a shriek
like a train whistle.

'It's disgusting. A cat in a bed. I never heard of such a
thing.'

'Then you never heard of cats.'

'You're quite rude.' Valentina herself, who was only an
aunt by marriage, was always quite rude to Carrie. That was
different.

'I'm only telling you.' Carrie Fielding had still not
stopped trying to give grown-ups bits of information they
did not want. 'Ages ago, cats lived in caves. They always
look for a cave. That's why they go into brown paper bags,
and in the drawers.'

'Don't tell me. I don't want to know!' Valentina turned
up her eyes and put her hand where she thought her heart
was – too low down, nearer where her supper was. 'It's too
much. The four of you here – well, that's my duty, with
your father gone off like a pirate and your poor mother so
badly hurt in the fire. But all these animals . . . this private
zoo . . .' She moved about the room in her tight snakeskin
boots, tweaking, muttering, making a face at Carrie's under-
wear.

The white cat, Maud, stared at her from the top of the
chest of drawers, with all her paws folded underneath and
her furred hips sticking out.

'Get off there, you fat spoiled beast!' Aunt Val shook her
finger, with all the flashy rings.

'She can't hear you, you know.'

7

'It hears all right.'

'Don't you know a white cat with blue eyes is always deaf?'

'Blue, green, purple – I won't have it on my runners.' She took a swipe at Maud, who only had to open her mouth and hiss lazily to make Valentina jump back as if she had met a jungle lion.

To cheer her up, Carrie said from the bed, 'Lucky for you I haven't saved up enough for my horse yet.' Her horse money was tied into a sock and hidden inside a leaking teddy bear, one of the few things she had saved from the fire. 'A horse could have lived in your toolshed though. We could have cut the door, you see, so that the top half—'

'It's too much.' Valentina said this every day. 'I'm going mad.' She spun towards the door on her tightly-booted legs for which two pythons had shed their skins, tripped over a dog that looked like a shaggy rug and stumbled out, calling to Carrie's Uncle Rudolf. 'I am going mad – mad, I say!'

'How can she go when she's gone already?' Carrie's brother Tom came in, with a bowl full of bored fish.

'Why did Uncle Rudolf marry her?'

'No one else would.' Tom was sixteen. He could make his voice very deep and gloomy. 'And he had to marry someone so he wouldn't have to leave his money to poor relations like us.'

'I can do without his money.' Carrie sat up in bed and hugged her knees, hiding under a curtain of long sand-coloured hair. But she could have done with just a bit of it. So far, the sock inside the teddy bear had only enough for one leg of a horse – from the knee down.

'I can do without living in his house.' Tom kicked the bed, and the kitten made a small earthquake under the covers.

'Write to Dad.'

'I don't know where he is.'

'Let's tell Mum.'

'She's too ill. Be patient.' Tom strode about the room, knocking into things. He was tall and thin, with impatient arms and legs that could not keep still. 'We must be patient.'

8

Their younger sister Em came in from the bathroom, with her thick dark hair slicked down wet, carrying a large black cat in front of her like a tray.

'Don't carry Paul like that.' Carrie put back her hair to criticize.

'He likes it.' In a sentimental fit, Em had been christened Esmeralda, but she had called herself Em as soon as she found out what her name was. 'He likes everything I do. He sits on the edge of my bath and drinks the water. Yesterday, he fell in.' Em laughed. She had different ideas about animals. More tough and casual. But the cats understood her. She dropped the black cat from a height and he landed neatly on his four white feet and walked off with his tail up and his eyes round and green.

'That's cruel,' Carrie said.

Em pushed out the bottom half of her face into a terrible insulting shape.

'She's getting very difficult, that child.' Tom creased his forehead like a worried mother. He carried the fish through into the expensive tiled and carpeted bathroom and tipped them into Em's bathwater for a swim.

Last week, a pair of guppies had gone down the overflow. The sewers of London would become populated with guppies, and they would come flopping into the sink when you turned on a tap. In New York, there were alligators thrashing about under the city. People bought tiny baby ones in Woolworth's. When they began to grow, the people panicked and flushed them down the drains and the alligators went on growing in the sewers.

Michael, who was the youngest, came in like a bishop in a long towel bathrobe meant for a man. They had lost everything when their house caught fire, and although their aunt and uncle had bought clothes for them, Valentina's patience had run out before she finished outfitting Michael.

'Excuse me.' He stirred the dog Charlie with a towelled toe. '*She* says you must go down to the cellar.' Charlie thumped his tail without opening his eyes. He was a part poodle, part golden retriever, part hearthrug, who liked people better than dogs. 'It is your duty,' Michael told him.

9

That was one of Valentina's favourite sayings.

'It's worst for him,' Carrie said. '*She* kicks him under the table.'

'I kick her back,' said Michael. 'That's *my* duty.'

'When we're at school,' Carrie said, 'I think *She* ties him up, and the cats laugh at him.'

'I don't blame them.' Em always sided with the cats. 'They think he bit through that old electric wire and burned down our house.'

'After the fire . . .' Carrie said, looking through the wall at nothing. 'Do you remember? There was just the spine of the chimney and bits of burned framework, like ribs, and our rubbish heap. I did a picture at school of the black broken ribs and the tin cans. Miss Peake called it morbid. I called it "After the Fire".'

Two

After the fire, after they had stood on the potato patch in the rain and watched the firemen finish off with axes and hoses the bits of their home that the flames had not destroyed, the Fielding children had been taken to Uncle Rudolf's house in London.

Tom was not a child. The others, Carrie, Em and Michael, did not feel like children that night. They had stood shivering in the mud, with the dog and the cats and the fish and the box of the hibernating turtle. And nobody else. Their mother had been taken away to hospital in the ambulance, because a falling beam had broken her back. Their father was sailing round the world in a home-made boat. They did not know how far he had got. He had not come home for nearly a year. Now there was no home for him to come to.

Uncle Rudolf was his elder brother who had made good and made money and made his name in plumbing. 'The

Prince of Plumbers', he was called in the trade. His brother Jerome, the children's father, called him The Baron of Bathwater. He called the children's father a Salted Seanut who had never provided for his wife and family. 'And don't come to me begging for a loan.'

When the house (which was only a glorified Army hut) had gone up in smoke, and Mum had been rushed off to hospital, and Tom, Carrie, Em and Michael and the animals were standing in the mud of the potato patch, the people who had come to see the marvellous spectacle of someone else's home going up in smoke began to say, 'What's to be done with the children? Where are the children to go?' Looking at each other to see if someone else would say, 'I'll take them in.'

There were so many of them . . . and all those pets . . . and the little boy seemed to have something wrong with his leg. He walked up and down, as if he had one foot on the pavement and one in the gutter.

'Where are your relations?' one of the policemen asked Tom.

'Haven't got any.' They hadn't really, except miles away in America, some unknown cousins. Uncle Rudolf didn't count. He had washed his hands of them when their father built the boat in the kitchen of the house where they used to live, and sailed away from Bristol. He had washed his hands again when their mother sold what was left of the house after knocking down walls to get the boat out, and moved the family to the old Army hut, and went out to work cooking and cleaning.

'Everybody has relations.' The policeman chewed on his shiny black chin strap. 'Haven't you got even *one*?'

'Well . . .' Tom had looked at Carrie, squatting in the mud with her dog, her wet hair salty in her mouth. At Em, who was said to be 'tough', wearing a soaked cat on her shoulders like an old fur collar, trying to be tough, with her jaw stuck out like a chimpanzee and her hyacinth-blue eyes angry. At small Michael, who had given up, and was crying into the fish bowl. 'Well . . . there is Uncle Rudolf.'

Uncle Rudolf did not want them, but when the policeman

11

rang him up in the middle of the night, he could not very well say, 'I have washed my hands of them.'

So they had been taken to the big red brick house in North London that Uncle Rudolf had bought when he made his money. A fitting palace for the Prince of Plumbers. He had painted all the gutters and drainpipes silver, to show them off. There were stained-glass windows and turrets and pinnacles and pillars twisted like barley sugar, and balconies that were forbidden to the children, and a garden as tidy as a public park that was forbidden to the animals after Charlie dug up a bed of Bleeding Heart.

Uncle Rudolf was a tall cold man with marble fingers and a bald head and smooth face like the stone egg Dad had sent home from the Canary Islands.

'If you can't eat it, sit on it,' Dad's note had said. 'You might hatch out a canary.'

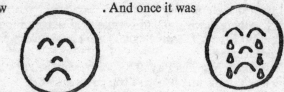

If he sent a damp splinter of wood or a shred of sailcloth, as he sometimes did, to prove disaster had struck. He drew . And once it was

when he ran aground in the delta of the Ganges.

Uncle Rudolf had married late in life this foolish woman Valentina, who invited people to lunch or tea or cocktails every day, so as to have someone to listen to her complaints. Uncle Rudolf had stopped listening long ago, and the children had never begun.

After the others had gone to their rooms, Carrie lay in

12

bed with the striped kitten curled on the pillow. It was called Nobody, because it would not take any of the names they tried. Valentina was banging about on the piano downstairs to prove that she could have been a concert pianist if only it had not been her duty to marry a plumber with four homeless nephews and nieces.

Carrie pulled the kitten closer to her ear, to drown out the piano with the purr which shook its small body. It had not yet grown up to the size of its motor.

She closed her eyes and waited to hear the movement of wind outside her window and the hollow beat of hooves on the road down from the stars.

Every night since she could remember, she had lain in bed wherever she was – in the house with the boat in the kitchen, in the Army hut, in this dark bedroom at Uncle Rudolf's that never got a smell of sun – and called, 'Penny-Come-Quick!' And he had come to her.

Penny-Come-Quick was a silver-grey Arab whose picture she had once cut out of a newspaper, galloping into the wind with his mane and tail floating as if he was flying. The picture had been lost long ago (Carrie lost everything, even her treasures), but the horse remained. Every night he came to her window, wherever she was, and although her body lay in bed, her real self slid on to his white satin back and he turned and galloped away with her.

Tonight he arched his neck, strong and warm under her hands, then threw up his head as the wind lifted his mane, and pawed at the night.

'Come on, Penny!' She felt his muscles gather beneath her, and he bounded away. Up and away to the star where all the famous horses of history grazed in the Elysian Fields, and all the horses and ponies that had been very much loved on earth waited for their own people to die, and come to call them at the gate.

Three

Next day after school, Carrie and Tom went to see their mother. The two younger ones were not allowed to visit the hospital.

'As if being young was an infectious disease,' Em grumbled. Her dark hair was made of curl springs. To tame it, she wore a sock tied round her forehead like an Indian, and grumbled from under that.

They all hated the school where they had to go now. Before the fire, they had gone to the small local school where everybody knew everybody and the teachers called you Dearie. But Uncle Rudolf, Prince of Plumbers, sent them to the grand new school at the top of the hill, with glass walls and shapeless statues and announcements booming out of loudspeakers instead of pinned up on a bulletin board. They did not know anybody and the work was different.

'Too difficult for you?' Aunt Valentina asked with glee.

'No. Different.'

At first, people at the new school had stared and asked questions and said, 'That's a lie,' to the answers. Then they only stared. Now they did not even stare. Tom, Carrie, Em and Michael were swallowed up in the great clattering mob of Londoners, and some of the teachers had not even learned their names.

Michael had hardly said a word since he had been there. He couldn't read aloud – at least, not the same words as other people – but was not going to let them know it. He wore his right hand in a sling, pretending it was sprained. He couldn't spell, but was not going to let them know it.

Tom waited for Carrie in the playground among the ugly statues that had holes in them, like Gorgonzola cheese. They stuffed their ugly green uniform cap and beret into the pockets of their ugly green blazers and went on a bus to the hospital, which was in the town near where they had lived in the old Army hut. After the first time they had been allowed to visit their mother, Carrie had dreamed about it for nights, and even Penny could not gallop her way from the frightening dreams. Now she and Tom were getting used to seeing their mother in her white plaster cast like a mummy case, with her thick fair hair tied back with a bit of bandage.

They waited in the corridor with the husbands and relations and friends of the other women in the ward until the swing doors opened at exactly six o'clock.

'Your mother is sleeping.' The Staff Nurse saw Tom and Carrie come in. She did not need to put out a hand to stop them. Her voice did it for her.

'Can we just go and look at her?' When Tom wanted his voice to be deep and grown up, it always came out cracked and high.

'Don't wake her.' Perhaps the nurse smiled at home, but she was not going to risk it at the hospital. 'She's been very difficult today.' This nurse was the one who said, 'Brace up now, Mrs Fielding. There's no reason for tears.'

The other one, who wasn't here today, the small fat one with the little teeth like pearl barley, said, 'Oh, poor Tom and Carrie. Oh, poor Mrs Fielding. I'm *so* sorry for you. It's not fair to have to suffer after you were so brave.'

Tom and Carrie stood on either side of the bed and looked down at their pale, sleeping mother. Her face looked smaller and the mouth that smiled and laughed and made jokes out of mistakes and disappointments was drawn thin and without colour.

'Difficult!' Carrie whispered. 'You can see she's been in pain.'

Huge warm tears came up from nowhere and flooded her eyes. She hung her head so that her hair swung forward, because the curious woman in the next bed was making her husband look, and saying, 'Ah, the poor kids. Ah, it's a rotten shame.'

The tears ran in through the small holes in the corner of Carrie's eyes and came down her nose. She wiped it on the back of her hand.

'She saved Mike's life, you know,' Tom said. He kept on saying this about their mother, as if he could not get over it.

Whether Charlie had bitten through the wire or not, it was his barking that woke them to the fumes of smoke and the crackle of flames. They had all run out of the house into what they called the garden. Michael had fallen.

'Where's Mike?'

They heard him scream inside the house. The doorway where they had run out leaped into a frame of fire. Their mother smashed a window with a stone, climbed through into a room full of smoke, and pushed Michael out of the window. As she came through herself, with glowing smoke reaching out hands to clutch her, the window frame and part of the wall collapsed on her, and when Tom and Carrie dragged her out on to the trodden mud, she was unconscious.

They would never forget it. 'She saved Mike's life,' Tom kept saying, though not any more in front of Valentina, because she replied, 'And look where it's got her.'

'What – what?' Their mother's eyes moved like marbles under the closed lids, then she blinked and woke up. 'What's that?'

'You saved Mike's life.'

'Did I?' She was doped and hazy. She was no more surprised to see her children than if they had been there when she fell asleep. Her burned hands lay outside the bedclothes in huge padded bandages, like white boxing gloves.

'Are you all right, my dears?' When she smiled up at them, the lines of pain spread and lifted into the mouth they knew.

'Of course. Everything's fine.' They began to make up some good things to tell her about school, and Em and Mike and the animals.

'Carrie's been crying,' their mother said when they finished.

'I'm all *right*!' Carrie said fiercely. 'We've told you – we're all *right*!'

16

Four

But they were not all right, of course. They were all wrong. Unhappy, each in their different way, and Uncle Rudolf and Aunt Valentina were unhappy too.

Fights sprang up all over the house. Angry shouts. Yells. Shrieks of chair legs as someone jumped up from a meal and went off to sulk. Banging doors. 'I'm going mad!' And a crashing of bass thunder on the piano.

Even the cats fought, up and down the stairs, in and out of the cupboards, along the tops of coat hangers and curtain rods, squalling and scattering lumps of white, black and tiger fur.

How long could this go on? One Sunday at a breakfast of toast and jam, because Maud, the deaf white cat had stolen the butter, and Carrie had dropped the dish of scrambled eggs on the carpet, Uncle Rudolf said, 'I think we all need a day out.'

He spoke in his usual cold, careful voice, but his smooth egg face looked as if it might crack under the strain.

'Outings cost money.' Sunday was Valentina's worst day. She always came back cross from church, as if the devil was angry with her for going.

'Not this one. Remember those sunken baths I made, with the mermaid tiles and the silver taps like dolphins? The customer can't pay the bill, so he's given me an old place he has in the country. Used to be an inn, but they made a new road, so no one came that way any more.'

After the usual commotion about whether the animals could come (they couldn't), and whether Valentina should invite her sad friend Rose Arbuckle who never had any fun (she invited her), they all got into the car. After the usual argument about which way to go, they turned on to a new fast, wide road where everybody seemed to be out on this

17

sunny summer Sunday. Valentina kept telling Uncle Rudolf how to drive.

'Don't pass. Watch that woman – she drives like a fool. Look out! Slow down. Go faster. Don't go so fast . . .'

'Stop breathing,' Tom murmured, wedged in the back seat with his brother and sisters. In the front, half smothered by Valentina's floating fox fur, poor Rose Arbuckle sat and sighed for the good old days and sniffed at the drop on the end of her long sad nose.

'Turn now!' Valentina, reading the map upside down, called out much too late. Uncle Rudolf cut across two lines of furious cars and they turned off the road and went round the edge of a hill where new red brick houses covered the slope like measles.

'Now that's what I like to see in the country.' Valentina was pleased for the first time that day. 'A little progress and civilization.' She stopped looking out of the window when they left the housing estates and drove through some quiet old villages, forgotten or never known by the people who raced along the new road, staring straight ahead.

'Uncle Rhubarb?'

'Don't call me that, Michael.'

'Can I open the window?' That meant Michael was going to be sick.

'No.' Valentina pulled the beautiful dead fox close round her neck at the mere thought of fresh air.

'You'll be sorry,' Carrie said. Michael was already green. Or was it the reflection from the tunnel of green leaves they were going through? It was a tall wood, arching over the road. The trees had smooth cool trunks with initials and hearts carved in them, and flat grey branches shaped like horses' necks.

The road was rutted and puddled. 'I hope we're nearly there.' Uncle Rudolf winced as his expensive car went in and out of a muddy hole. 'This must be the wood. It used to be called Wood's End Inn. When they built the new road, and no travellers came this way any more, the local people started to call it World's End.'

The end of the world . . . Coming out of the wood into

sudden sunlight, the old road took a turn round an over-grown hedge full of wild roses, and there it was.

It was a stone house with a tiled roof dipping in the middle and curling at the edges. It was very shabby, with damp green patches on the walls, broken windows, and rooks flying out of the chimneys. The path to the door was made of great flat millstones, grown over with grass and weeds, with half a millstone for the doorstep. There were two rotting, rickety benches where old men must have once sat outside with mugs of beer, and the old inn sign still swung, creaking and crooked, with all the paint peeled off.

Tom and Carrie and Em and Michael stared from the car. Michael did not feel sick any more.

'It's beautiful.' Carrie got out on to the wet grass, staring at the house. The sweet air filled her head like a song. 'Why don't you come and live here, Uncle Rudolf?'

'My dear child, you must be insane.' He leaned a hand on her shoulder while he put on his galoshes. 'In this dead place?'

But the house was not dead. Only asleep.

At one side, there was a gate that had once been white, off its hinges and leaning against the tilted gatepost. Beyond it, a grass-grown yard and some outbuildings. A big thatched barn with holes in the boards and the black paint weathered to grey. An open cart shed. A low line of stables with half doors and a crooked straw roof. Everything old and worn and comfortable, as if it had never been built, but had grown up out of this soft ground, centuries ago.

Moving like a sleepwalker, Carrie climbed over the gate and went across the yard, with her eyes on the stables. The top half of one door was open. She looked inside. There was still some old straw bedding on the uneven floor. A hay rack. An iron manger in the corner, everything draped with dust and cobwebs, everything long ago abandoned. But . . . she breathed in deeply and shut her eyes. The smell of a horse was still there.

In the open shed, there was an old dog-cart, leaning down on its shafts, the lamp glass broken, the seat mildewed, and white with the droppings of swallows, who had made a

They all stared from the car

whole village of dried mud nests in the rafters above.

Hanging on the wall were some pieces of harness. Cracked reins, a rusted bit, a collar with the lining rotted and the straw coming out. Carrie put her face against it, and nodded. Yes. The smell of a horse was for ever.

She took down the collar and hung it round her neck, and stepped between the shafts of the brown dog-cart and lifted them up.

She might have stood there all day, ready to trot out, arching her neck to the imagined feel of the bit and reins, but they were yelling for her from the hill behind the house. She could see them going up through the long grass of the neglected meadow. Tom and Em carried the picnic basket, pulling it from side to side, as if they were arguing. Uncle Rudolf plodded with his galoshes and a stout stick, as if he were going up Mount Everest. Valentina and Rose Arbuckle staggered in tight skirts and silly town shoes, leaning on each other and giving out wails and complaints that Carrie could hear from the yard.

She hung up the collar and raced round the back of the house, past some tumbledown hen houses and what might once have been a garden, with one six-foot sunflower growing out of the weeds. She caught up with the others on the grassy hill. Michael was limping more than usual on the rough ground.

'Head up, boy!' Uncle Rudolf called in the voice left over from his Army days. 'Walk like a man.'

'I am, Uncle Rhubarb.'

'Don't call me that.'

'He can't help it,' Tom said. Everyone knew that, but Uncle Rudolf, who did not often laugh, was always afraid that someone might laugh at him.

'And stop limping,' he grumbled.

'He can't help it,' Tom said patiently. 'One leg is shorter than the other.'

'The doctors fixed that years ago,' said Uncle Rudolf.

'They did the wrong leg.'

'Nonsense,' Uncle Rudolf said briskly. 'The limp has become a habit, that's all.'

21

'Playing for sympathy.' Valentina panted up, dragging Rose Arbuckle, who wished she hadn't come. 'People who want sympathy never get it.'

'So I see,' Tom said.

Carrie said, 'In case you'd like to know, the Queen's great-grandmother, Queen Alexandra was her name, had a stiff knee from a child. But she limped so gracefully that all the fashionable ladies copied it. The Alexandra limp, they called it. In case you'd like to know.'

'Yes, yes, I know,' Valentina said irritably. She didn't know, but you could never tell her anything.

'Let's stop here.'

'No, here.'

'No, farther on.'

'No, there under that tree.'

'No, at the top of the hill!' Swinging the basket, the children ran ahead, away from the usual picnic argument, and stopped in a line by the fence at the top of the meadow. On the slope below, a herd of cows grazed on the sweet tufted grass, heads all pointed the same way, like a tidy child's toys. The bramble thicket at the edge of the wood ran up the hill and down the other side to where the curve of a stream was marked by pollard willows. And beyond, the patchwork greens and browns and yellows of the summer fields of England.

Five

'You shouldn't have brought me.' Rose Arbuckle was limping worse than Michael, her ankles turning at every step like a bad skater. 'All my life I've been a drag on people.'

'Rubbish.' Valentina let her fall at the top of the hill, gave one insulting glance at the splendid view and demanded, 'Where's the beer?'

Where's the beer! The grown-ups would not look at the

view. They sat on a blanket and unpacked the lunch and complained because there was no salt for the hard-boiled eggs.

Uncle Rudolf grumbled about the bad bargain he had got in exchange for his sunken baths with the mermaid tiles and dolphin taps.

'No use to me. A white elephant of a place, this is. Never sell it. World's End is right. What a ruin. Haunted, I shouldn't wonder.' His big yellow tombstone teeth tore at a chicken drumstick.

'Br-r-r-r.' Valentina swallowed beer and shuddered and pulled the fox fur closer round her neck, although it was a warm day and she was sweating under her thick make-up. 'Spooky old end of nowhere.'

As Carrie looked back at the house below them, hunching its shoulders, unwanted, a cloud of birds rose up above the chimneys like smoke, as if there *was* someone in there, stirring up the fire. Slitting her eyes to blur them out of focus, for a moment she could imagine she saw a phantom face at one of the windows, a ghostly hand raised to draw back the tattered curtain. She opened her eyes and the window was black and empty, the rags of curtains hanging still.

'Sit down and don't be so restless,' Uncle Rudolf told her. 'You'll get indigestion.'

'It's better for your stomach to move about,' Carrie said. 'At Roman banquets, they used to run round the table between each course, and then be sick to make more room.'

'Go away,' Valentina said, and Rose Arbuckle moaned, 'That's done it. I can't eat another thing.'

Carrie took her sandwich up to the fence, and she and Tom watched a man on a horse cantering through the water meadows on the other side of the stream. It was a big bay horse with the swinging stride of a thoroughbred, its hooves raising a fine silvery mist from the wet grass.

'*I stand and look at them long and long . . .*' Tom said.

'What's that?'

'A poem. *I think*, it says, *I think I could turn and live with animals—*'

('Oh *so* could I!' Carrie said.)

23

'They are so placid and self-contained.
I stand and look at them long and long.
They do not sweat and whine about their condition—'
('Like some we could mention.')
'They do not lie awake in the dark and weep for their sins.'
('I bet Rose Arbuckle does.')
'They do not make me sick discussing their duty to God . . .'

'Yes. Aunt Val makes me sick,' Carrie whispered. 'Does she you?'

'Hush.' Tom smiled, watching the man and the horse jump over a ditch and splash a dark track away across the shining field. 'She is very good to us. It is her duty.'

It was Aunt Val's duty to go back to London early, before anyone had had a chance to explore, or to see if they could get into the house. She was having what she called a Fork Supper, which meant that the guests had to stand about uncomfortably with a glass and a plate, wishing they had a third hand for the fork. Or had to put down the glass and poke at the food without being able to cut it. Or had to sit with the plate on their knee and try to keep the sauce out of their laps.

Carrie and Em had to wear skirts and be waitresses. Em did not mind so much, since she quite liked to dress up and pretend to be somebody else, smiling her big white teeth at the guests and hearing them tell each other, 'What a lovely child! Those eyes! Like an Italian sky.' (To show they'd been to Italy.)

Carrie's eyes were the ordinary greenish-brown kind that go with sandy hair that gets mud-coloured if you don't wash it. For the Fork Supper, she had to tie it back, which she hated, since it gave her face no protection from the guests, who either looked through her as if she were invisible, or asked pointless questions like 'Do you like school?' and turned away without waiting for an answer.

She took a dish of creamed chicken out to the kitchen before the guests had a chance at seconds, and all the children fell on it with their fingers.

24

Valentina caught them at it. 'Oh, it's too, too much! I'm going mad. I shall have to tell your uncle.' She huffed to the door, lifting her lizard skin shoes over the bodies of Charlie and the three cats, who always lay in the middle of the kitchen floor to make sure of being noticed. In a shoebox on top of the refrigerator was a stray kitten they had found in the hen house at World's End and brought home hidden inside Tom's shirt. It was orange coloured, so they called it Pip.

'Too many of these beastly animals—' Valentina did not even know about Pip.

'Not enough,' Carrie said, licking her fingers. 'If only we lived in the country, we'd have dozens and dozens.'

'Oh! I can't stand any more! Oh, it's hard on me!'

'They do not sweat and whine about their condition.' Tom quoted the poem softly, as the kitchen door swung angrily behind her. *'I think I could turn and live with animals . . .'*

Six

They had all had the same idea. They fought as much as any family, and screamed and punched and sometimes bit, and told Charlie, 'Kill her! Attack!' while he smiled and thumped his tail and rolled his mild eyes, but when there was a good idea about, they all grabbed it together.

After school, they met in the playground among the Gorgonzola statues, and went out by bus to the depressing grey suburb where Uncle Rudolf had his plumbing factory. It was no use trying to talk to him at home, with Valentina flouncing about in clothes made of dead animals and talking about herself.

The factory was an old-fashioned building of dirty yellow brick, with spiked iron railings all round, like a prison. Over the great studded door, Uncle Rudolf had put a royal emblem of a huge crown and crossed water pipes, with a Latin motto: 'Princeps Plumbarium'. The Prince of Plumbers.

Tom and Carrie and Em and Michael had been there before when Uncle Rudolf had given them a tour of the workshops where pipes were elbowed into strange angles, and baths beaten into shape with hollow clangs. He had hoped to interest one of them into coming into the plumbing business some day. That was before he had to have them living in his house. Now he would not have had them as a gift.

'What's this?' he asked irritably, as the four of them, having waited for his secretary to go and get her tea, charged into his office and stood on the carpet before his desk.

'It's a delegation,' said Tom.

'Well, I haven't time.' Uncle Rudolf had actually been reading a magazine when they came in, but he began to push papers and bits of broken pipe and strings of washers about, to look busy.

'But this may be the happiest day of your life,' Carrie said.

'The happiest day of my life will be when I can get some peace to do my work.'

'Ah,' said Tom, shifting his bony weight from one long leg to the other, like a horse. 'That's just it.'

'We've had an idea,' Carrie said.

Em said nothing. She had learned from the cats to wait and be cautious.

'A brilliant idea, Uncle Rhubarb.' Michael stepped forward and put his chewed fingertips on the desk and his head on one side. He could look horrible when he was dirty, with his clothes sagging at the waist and falling off his shoulders and his hair like scarecrow straw, but he was still young enough to be able to turn on the charm like one of Uncle Rudolf's taps. The innocent, babyish charm that the others had exchanged for growing years.

'Don't call me that,' Uncle Rudolf said, but at least he listened to the idea. He listened, but he did not like it.

'But you've got the house!' they cried. 'You said you

couldn't sell it, and it's going to waste with nobody in it.'

'It's going to pieces.'

'We could fix it up. We could live there.'

'What on?' Uncle Rudolf laughed without mirth.

'I'm seventeen,' Tom said. 'Well – sixteen then. In my seventeenth year. I can leave school. I can get a job. I'm not a child.'

'You talk like one.' Uncle Rudolf pushed his lips in and out like a windy baby. 'It's impossible. You'd starve to death. I'd have the authorities on me for child neglect.' He seemed to care more about that than the starving.

'If that's what's worrying you . . .' Em had kept quiet, watching all the faces, the eager begging young ones and the cold, scoffing older one, set years ago in the shape of disapproval. 'Why not give us the money it costs you to keep us now?'

Uncle Rudolf was very fond of his money. He did not like other people to talk about it. He got up behind the desk angrily, but Em licked a finger to flatten a curl on her cheek and said calmly, 'Isn't it worth your while to pay us to keep out of your way? A business deal.'

Worth his while . . . Business deal . . . That was the sort of talk the Prince of Plumbers understood.

Aunt Valentina, of course, was delighted, although she pretended that she would miss them.

'You can come and visit us,' Michael said kindly.

'I shall do that, of course. It will be my duty.'

Their father was still somewhere at sea, or holed up in a café in some fishing port he had taken a fancy to, from where he would eventually send them a postcard: 'Paradise on earth. All fly out next plane.' But with no address and no mention of who would pay the fare.

There remained only their mother. Tom and Carrie stood on either side of her high hospital bed, while the curious woman in the next bed tried to hear what they were saying, and their mother moved her eyes restlessly back and forth, since she could not toss in her plaster cast, nor even turn her head, which was wedged with sandbags.

27

'I don't know,' she worried. 'I don't know.'

'Yes you do. You know we'll be all right. Haven't we always been all right? Weren't we all right the night the storm blew the roof off when you were out washing up at the railwaymen's banquet? Weren't we all right when the burglar came and we locked him in the cellar?'

'He was the gas meter man, not a burglar.'

'But if he had been. Don't you trust us? Oh Mum, it's such a Place. The World's End ... But there's a school in the next village but one, a small school that looks like the kind of place where you can get sums wrong without being told your life is a total disaster. And when you get out of hospital you can come and live there.'

'I won't be able to walk or do anything for ages.' Poor active, lively Mum, who never used to sit down all day until she fell exhausted into bed. Why didn't broken backs happen to people like Rose Arbuckle, who would enjoy the excuse to do nothing?

'We'll put your bed under a window that looks out on the meadow, and you can watch the horses.'

'Will there be horses?' She looked at Carrie.

'There will if it kills me.'

That night, Carrie lay in bed and heard Aunt Val playing tinkly piano music – she was happy now – and heard the stir of wind and the sound of his galloping hooves. The grey Arab trod the air outside her window, his large dark eyes like liquid velvet. She rose in her waking dream and slid on to his back.

'Soon.' She stroked the flat arch of his neck. 'Soon, Penny, I'll call you from the World's End. Will you come to me there?'

He blew warm breath into the night, wanting to go.

'There's a stable there. I'll clean it out and whitewash it and put down fresh straw. Even if I never do get a horse, I can be with you there. At the end of the world.'

Aunt Val began to sing, gargling the high notes. Michael cried out in his sleep, and somewhere on some garden wall, some cat howled like a wolf. Penny-Come-Quick turned and galloped away into the sky.

In the Elysian Fields that night, Carrie met Bucephalus, the battle charger of Alexander the Great. 'I never let anyone else ride me.' He had been telling his proud story for two thousand years. 'Only the conqueror of the world.'

'Wasn't much of a world in those days.' Clever Hans, the Talking Horse who had once made a living doing arithmetic problems, was bored by war horses. 'If they sailed out of the Mediterranean Sea, they thought they'd drop off the edge.'

Penny wandered about, nodding to friends, nibbling a neck as he passed, dropping his delicate head to graze on the sweetest grass in the Universe. Sitting loosely on his back, her fingers twined in his silken mane, Carrie met a Derby winner, and Black Bess, who had carried the highwayman Dick Turpin, and a small blind costermonger's pony who was waiting for the old man who had bought oats for his feedbag when he had no bread himself, and covered him with his own coat when it rained.

Carrie told them about the house at World's End, and how she and Tom and Em and Michael were going to make it their place, to live their kind of way.

'I think I could turn and live with animals . . .' She quoted the poem to them. They were quite interested.

Seven

They moved in as soon as the summer term was over.

Uncle Rudolf bought them sleeping-bags and tin mugs and plates and an iron kettle and cooking pot, since at first it would be more like camping out than living in a house. Aunt Val gave them fly spray and a half-gallon bottle of Milk of Magnesia, and a lot of advice about wet feet and not letting a dog lick your face.

Nobody listened. They were not listening to any voice

from the past. They had their ears pricked forward to the new adventure ahead.

Carrie wanted to throw away her hateful school uniform, but Tom, who had suddenly become very grown up, said No. There might be lean times coming. They would need every stitch next winter.

'Not my gym tunic.'

'Em can make it into a skirt.' Em could sew. Their mother's sewing machine, an indestructible heap of old iron, had been one of the few things saved from the fire.

'If you're going to order everyone about and tell them what to do, I'm not coming,' Em said. 'And nor are the cats.'

But someone had to be head of the house, and Tom was the eldest, and he wasn't going back to school next year (although his mother thought he was). The first night at World's End, when they had considered the bedrooms, with their bird's nests and their few sagging old bits of furniture and their windows broken by village boys, Carrie and Em had been glad when Tom decided they should all sleep downstairs. And when they had blown out the candles and lay in their sleeping-bags on the flagstone floor of the front room which had once been the lounge of the Wood's End Inn, they were both very glad to have Tom there to say, in his deepest voice, 'Don't worry. Old houses always creak.'

'But it's outside, Tom,' Michael said. 'It's – it's trying to get in.'

'If you're going to get hysterical, the very first night—'

'I am not historical. There's somebody crying outside.'

'A dog,' Tom said.

'A cat?' But Carrie knew that all the cats were in. Maud and Paul and Nobody and the stray orange kitten they had found on the day of the picnic.

'A lost baby . . .' Michael whispered. 'The ghost of a baby looking for the churchyard . . .'

'It's the inn sign creaking over the door,' Em grunted. 'Shut up and let a person sleep.'

The creak-squeak of the sign in the wind was now quite friendly. But that other sound . . . inside the house. On the staircase. 'Old houses always creak,' Tom had said. But he could say what he liked. There was no doubt about it. There *was* someone on the stairs.

When the others had fallen asleep at last, and Carrie lay awake, wishing she could make a hole for her hip in the floor, like you can in the sand, someone – something – tiptoed up the stairs. Quite slowly. Step by step.

'What's that?' she shouted, and everyone sat up. Charlie barked once, a shrill, aimless bark, then dropped his head again.

'I'm going to see.' Since Tom was head of the house, he had to say that, and since he said it, Carrie had to say, 'I'll come with you. Charlie?' He would not even get up. Why didn't he whine and raise his hackles, as dogs were supposed to do when they smelled ghosts? Life was not like books.

Tom lit the stub of a candle. Carrie walked behind him with her hand over her eyes, looking through her fingers as if she were watching a horror film. They opened the door to the narrow hall. There was another door opposite which still said 'Public Bar', a passage leading back to the kitchen and store rooms, and the wide stairs going straight up at the end of the hall.

Tom walked towards the stairs bravely, but Carrie knew his bony shoulders and the knobby back of his neck well enough to know that he was scared. He raised the candle. The flame blew in a draught from a broken window. Shadows moved on the staircase, but there was no one there. Then as they stood in the dark hall and looked up, they heard three more footsteps towards the top of the stairs. *But there was no one there.*

For a moment, Tom and Carrie still stood staring up, with their mouths open. Then they looked at each other. Then without a word, they ducked back into the front room.

The four of them spent the rest of the night keeping the fire and the candles going. They didn't talk. They listened. They heard no more footsteps, but they all knew, without having to discuss it, that they could not stay another night in this house.

Their short sweet dream was over already. Their beautiful

World's End was a place of nightmare and terror. Carrie sat stiffly with her back against a table leg and her arm round Charlie's fur shoulders. It was the first night for ages that she did not even think about calling the Arab horse. She was much too frightened.

When the first light of dawn began to spread through the small panes of the old leaded windows and across their tired faces, things began to look better.

'Perhaps we imagined it,' Tom said. He had been to the back of the house to fill the kettle, and had found nothing strange. No trail of blood on the stairs. No feeling of ice-cold fear in the passage, or in the raftered, stone-floored kitchen with its low sink as big as a small bathtub and its ancient round scarred table, cut with the initials of people who had lived there.

'Who's going up to look?' Em asked, getting back into her sleeping-bag and curling like a maggot.

No one offered. If anybody – or anything – had gone up in the night to those cold, cobwebby bedrooms, nobody wanted to see it.

'Because I know there's nothing there,' Tom argued. 'Let's give it one more night.'

'No.' Em stuck her jaw out over the edge of the sleeping-bag. 'You can't make us.'

Michael said, 'I'm not afraid. But the girls are.'

Carrie said, 'No, Tom. It's not fair on the younger ones.' She was not going to tell them about the face she had imagined at the window on the day of the picnic. The footsteps on the stairs were enough without that. Because now she was beginning not to be sure whether she had imagined the white face, or actually seen it.

'But where could we go?' Tom poured out the tea. Ashes had got into the kettle. It tasted disgusting. 'We can't go back to Uncle Rudolf's.' As soon as they had left, Valentina had filled their rooms with a whole rabble of her nastiest relations, to make Uncle Rudolf feel that *his* family had been keeping *hers* out. 'We'd have to camp out.'

'Or sleep in the stable,' Carrie said. 'If we could only get a horse before winter it would be warm.'

'Oh, knock it off,' Tom said irritably. He liked horses. They all liked horses. But Carrie overdid it.

Michael began to wail. He was hungry, and he wouldn't drink tea without milk. 'I want to go home!'

'This is your home, boy.' Em's hair had been especially wild and wiry when she crawled out of her sleeping-bag. To flatten it, she had pulled a red woollen cap low down on her forehead. Her deep blue eyes stared under it at Michael. 'There's nowhere else to go.'

'What are we going to doo-oo-oo?' Michael went on wailing.

Tom put his hands to the sides of his head. 'I don't know,' he said crossly. 'Shut up. I don't know.'

'Some head of a house,' Em jeered.

'If you want orders,' Tom told her, 'go to the village and get us some milk, and something to eat.'

'Make Carrie go.'

'I don't want to.'

'You can both go then.'

They did not want to go together, or alone. No one wanted to do anything. It was all spoiled. Their wonderful idea of living here, of living the way they wanted to without grown-ups to interfere, of making the poem come true: *I think I could turn and live with animals . . .*

They went outside on to the uncut grass, dewed with morning cobwebs, and looked glumly at the old stone house. It stared back at them glumly with its cracked windows, an upstairs blind hanging halfway down crookedly, like a drooping eyelid. They felt just as miserable and rejected as when they had stood on the potato patch in the rain and looked at the black ruin of their Army hut. Once more, they had no one to turn to, nowhere to go.

Eight

Carrie and Em dragged their feet up the lane, in the other direction from the wood. Over the rise of a small hill was the village where there were a few shops, and a church, and some houses and cottages full of people they would now never get to know.

The dairy was a white-painted shed at the back of a farm-house on the edge of the village.

'New round these parts?' Mr Mossman was as broad and heavy as one of his own milk churns. His wide red face was like the sinking sun, his hands were like hams, with sausages for fingers. His rubber boots were as wide as tree trunks, with thick ribbed soles that marked the ground like a tractor.

'We're the people at the World's End,' Carrie said, since Em was not going to answer. Em was still at the age when you can't make yourself speak to a stranger, or sometimes even someone you know.

'Oh, you're *those* people.' Mr Mossman nodded the tweed hat which sat too small on the top of his bushy grey head, with the brim turned up all round. He nodded several times, as if there had already been a lot of talk in the village. 'Yes, *that's* who you are,' he said, as if he were telling Carrie, not she telling him.

'Yes. I mean – well, we *were*, but—'

'Too far gone? Can't cope with such a blooming ruin?' Mr Mossman was good at putting words into other people's mouths. 'Well, I'll tell you what you do.' He folded his hands over the thick jersey that was stretched across his stomach like a jib sail full of wind. 'What you want to do is this . . .'

He began to lecture about shoring up and tamping down and reeving in and mucking out, but Carrie interrupted him. 'We can't,' she said shortly. 'It's haunted.'

'Oh, fish now, what's this? I know that old place. Used to

34

get my beer there when it was still in business. It's no more haunted than I am.'

'There's a ghost on the stairs.' Carrie watched to see if he would laugh.

He did laugh, but not a jeer. He opened his mouth very wide, like a split melon, and laughed through what were left of his teeth.

'Been like that for years, old chump! Poor old Neddy Drew, who was caretaker there, used to say it kept him company.'

'The ghost?' Em whispered, looking up at him from under the red wool cap.

'No, chump, the stairs! They're old, see. In the daytime, when it's warmer, the boards expand. Then at night they shrink away from the old loose nails. Crack, crack, crack.'

'How do you know?'

'My dear Miss What's-it,' Mr Mossman said, sticking out his front even farther and tilting the tweed hat over his grey forelock, which was like a Welsh pony, 'I know everything. Stay round here and you'll find *that* out.'

'Oh, we will, we will! Oh *thanks*.' Carrie and Em could not wait to get back and tell the others. They rushed out with the milk, and ran down the village street to the shops where they could buy bread and bacon and butter, and a stamp to write to their mother. They were stared at by the long-faced grocer, questioned by his sharp-eyed daughter, and tut-tutted at by the old lady in the post office, which was only a fire guard nailed to the counter in the sweet-shop.

'You really going to live in that old scarecrow of a place?' She took her spectacles out of the cash box to examine Carrie and Em better.

'Of course we are.'

'You *like* it out there?'

'We love it!'

On the way into the village, they had walked in silence, one in front of the other, kicking pebbles sulkily. Now they raced home, swinging shopping bags, laughing, throwing jokes, and the sun raced with them down the lane, sweeping

35

up cloud shadow, flooding the countryside with joy. Charlie ran back and forth like a maniac, travelling six times as far, leaping on and off banks with his legs thrown out like a steeplechaser, wriggling through hedges, leaving some of his wool behind like a sheep, galloping back to jump round them as they ran, his lip lifted in the famous giggly smile he inherited from his mother.

'We can stay!' Carrie and Em leaped the dry ditch at the edge of the lane and ran up the path of millstones, jumping from one to the other, and burst through the door with a shout. In the front room, Tom was rolling sleeping-bags and putting clothes back into cardboard boxes. He sat back on his heels while they told him about Mr Mossman. Slowly a grin spread over his face, and without a word, he stirred up the fire, unpacked the frying-pan and began to cook breakfast.

They worked all day in the house, beginning the enormous task of cleaning and repairing. Tom oiled the squeaky inn sign, and Michael went up a ladder, with half the rungs missing and painted the name on one side of the sign, and on the other side, a globe of the world with nothing on it but a little house with smoke going off into infinity.

World's End.

That night they sat round the fire and listened. Crack, crack, crack. The old boards of the staircase shrank and settled. Not ghostly. Friendly and comfortable. How could they have been so afraid?

'Let's sleep upstairs,' Tom said.

Em went ahead, carrying Paul like a tray, the fluffy white cat following with her trousers spread out like riding breeches. Michael was already asleep. Art work always wore him out.

Tom picked him up – 'Not scared, Carrie?'

'I shall never be frightened in this house again.'

Carrie's room was at the corner. One window looked out to the slope of the meadow, the other to the stable yard. When she got her horse, she would be within sight of him, wherever he was.

Tonight when she called, and Penny-Come-Quick came to

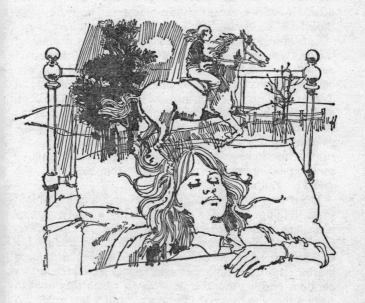

They galloped up the meadow . . .

her broken window, his nostrils square to the heady night smells of fields and wood, they did not take off for the stars. They galloped up the meadow, jumped the fence at the top, plunged down the other side, hopping the tussocks, took the wide stream like flying, and cantered off to explore the silver water meadows and the patchwork countryside, a new land under the moon.

Nine

There was so much work to do.

Tom puttied new glass into the windows and set some new tiles into the roof and painted the doors and window frames, none of which were at quite the same angle. The whole house leaned slightly inward from the edges, like a fat man's bed.

Em, who took after their mother in ways that had passed Carrie by, made an apron out of a feed sack and cleaned up the house, room by room. Tom said Carrie must help her, but Tom was out a lot, riding round the nearby villages and towns on an ancient fireman's bicycle known as Old Red, looking for a job. So Carrie spent most of her time in the barn and the stables, sweeping out, slopping on whitewash, patching up the worst holes. Often she just sat in the dusty straw or folded herself into a corner manger, with a book, or a dream of horses. If anyone called from the house, she yelled back, 'I'm busy!'

The thatched barn across the yard was full of marvellous wrecked things. A broken chaff-cutter like a giant's mincing machine. Plough handles with no blades. Bits of wheel-barrows, wheels, harness, a pile of rusted horseshoes big enough for a Clydesdale. At one end of the barn, steep narrow steps led to an open hayloft under the thatch, with a big door opening into the air, through which they used to unload the high haycarts. There were still a few mildewed bales of hay and straw, and a moulting cushion and some dishes and hard green lumps of bread, as if children had once played house up there.

Mr Mossman, the dairy farmer, grazed some of his cows in the tussocky field on the other side of the hill. He stopped in at World's End sometimes, to see what everyone was doing and tell them how to do it. When he found Carrie cementing the broken paving outside the stable, he told her that all her horses would get blood poisoning from the cement, first scratch they got.

'All my horses.' Carrie cut her initials with the trowel in the wet cement: C.F. and the outline of a horse's head, facing left, the only way she could draw them. 'I'll be lucky if I ever have *one*.'

'You'll be lucky if you *only* have one,' Mr Mossman said. 'No such thing as one horse, you know, like with peanuts or potato crisps. I've had 'em all. Shires, Shetlands, show jumpers, the lot. Every time the wife persuades me to give 'em up, someone comes along and begs me to take a pair of hunters for the season, or break a young 'un, or school a polo pony.'

This was hard to believe, since his ramshackle stable in the cow barn only housed a fat old porridge-coloured cob called Princess Margaret Rose, with a Roman nose and a back like a sofa.

'Best horse across country in her day,' Mr Mossman said. 'The owner wouldn't let no one else have the care of her. Horses come to you. They come to you, see, if you are a born horse fool.'

'They don't come to me.' Carrie's horses had all been in books, or in her head.

'They will, old dear. You're a horse fool. They'll come to you.'

'A grey Arab,' Carrie dreamed. 'Or a shining black thoroughbred with long sloping pasterns—'

'He'll go lame on you,' Mr Mossman warned.

'A bright bay with two white socks, a star, perhaps a narrow blaze, a little delicate head carried very high . . .'

'Neck set on upside down?' Mr Mossman asked suspiciously.

'Oh no, he'll have natural flexion. Like this.' She curved her chin down, mouthing an imaginary bit.

'You're over-flexing him,' Mr Mossman said sharply. He always had to know best, even about a dream horse.

When he came over the hill from his cow pasture one day and found Michael trying to cut the long grass behind the house with scissors, to make a place for a table and chairs, he said, 'You come along with me, old chump, and I'll loan you the world's finest lawnmower.'

The world's finest lawnmower turned out to be a brown Nubian goat on a chain, called Lucy, and a large sheep called Henry, who had been an orphan lamb, brought up as a pet. Reared on the bottle in Mr Mossman's kitchen, he grew up to think he was a dog. He wore a collar, ate dog biscuits, lay by the fire, chased cats, swam in the duck pond and in short, as Mr Mossman said, did everything but bark.

In the days when the World's End was an inn, Henry the ram used to follow Mr Mossman there, and push his way into the public bar for a taste of beer. So now when you went into the house, he was often behind you, shouldering his way through the door. Or if you opened the door to go outside, he would be standing there waiting to nip in before you could shut him out. He was as broad as a table, even when he was sheared. If he was standing still and thinking, Michael could put a plate on his woolly back and eat off it.

One day, Michael came back from the village with two chickens in a basket.

'Chicken stealing?' Tom peered. 'Where did you get those?' The hens hooded their flat round eyes shyly and chuckled inside their telescopic necks.

'Mr Mismo.'

'Who?'

'At the dairy, Mr Mismo.'

'You mean Mossman.'

'I call him Mismo.'

'That means "the same" in Spanish.'

'Well then, it's the same as Mossman. I met him when I was buying shop eggs and he said if I didn't eat new-laid eggs, I'd come all out in spots, so he gave me Diane and Currier.'

'Why Currier?'

'That's her name.'

So Michael was very busy too, cleaning out the hen house and planting a small dead tree in there for perches. Diane and Currier watched him labour to set it up for them, and then wouldn't sit in it. They perched on top of the laying boxes, and the orange cat, Pip, who had, after all, been found as a stray in this hen house, sat in the dead tree and stared at them.

With a bent hazel twig and a pencil, Michael fixed up the door of the old toolshed so that the goat could sleep in there, and also the ram, although Henry preferred the kitchen. Mr Mismo said they should be left out, 'Under the stars, where they was born', but Michael had heard footsteps on the cinder path one night, and seen footprints in the morning, and he was afraid of poachers.

Everyone was so busy in those first weeks at World's End that they had no time to find out if it was Charlie, or the cats, or the poachers who were stealing food. The end of a loaf of bread, a piece of cheese, a biscuit – things that were left out began to disappear. Then a piece of Sunday roast beef was suddenly gone. Too big for a cat to carry off, and Charlie had not had time to eat it or bury it.

He was lying under the round kitchen table, with his head hanging over a bar of the legs and his eyes turned up.

'Where's our lunch?' Carrie asked him.

He got up with a sigh, went to the rubbish bin and politely brought back a rotten tomato, holding it as gently as a bird dog.

'You see how clever? He could make his fortune on the stage. Now put it back, Charlie.'

He dropped the tomato in a squelchy mess on Carrie's foot, then bowed and grinned, with his front legs stretched out and his eyes rolled up. Unlike most dogs, the brown colour of his eyes did not fill the whole space. It showed white all round it, like a person.

Later that day, Carrie went up to the hay loft in the barn.

41

She opened the high loading door and made herself lean out and look down to get the lurching dizzy feeling, then lay down on a nest of dusty hay in the sun.

Who whined? Charlie would not climb the narrow steps since he had once slipped halfway up and fallen into a heap of chaff. Anyway he was out ram-watching. Beyond the roof of the house, Carrie could see him lying in the meadow with his head on his paws pointing to where Henry dozed under a tree, one as woolly as the other.

Another whine. It came from under the angle of the sloping roof. Carrie got up and went over. Behind a bale of straw lay a skeleton-thin dog, one side of its head caked with dried blood, as if it had been hit with a stick. On the floor was what looked like – no, was – their Sunday beef.

'So you took it, whoever you are.' Poor feeble dog, part terrier, part pointer, with a ratty tail and a harsh, filthy coat. A bitch, who looked as if she had recently had puppies to feed. Somehow she had dragged herself up the steps and then not even been able to eat the meat, only licked round it and chewed at the corners. She looked at Carrie without raising her head, her eye not trusting, but watching for the blow or the kick she had learned to expect from humans.

Carrie put her hand gently on the bony head. ('Never touch a strange dog,' Aunt Valentina's voice yapped in her memory.) The tail thumped feebly on the boards, and her heart went out to the dog in an agony of pity. She picked her up and carried her down the steps and into the house.

'She found us.' They made a bed for the dog near the stove and called her Perpetua, because she was a persecuted mother, like the saint in one of the old books they had found in the attic. 'She knew this was a refuge, so she came to us. And perhaps,' Carrie said, feeding the dog tiny bits of beef by hand, while Charlie watched in wonder, 'when she gets well, she'll go out and spread the tale that any animal in trouble can find shelter here.'

'Wouldn't it be wonderful,' Tom said, 'to have a – a sort of refuge, where animals could come that people had been cruel to.'

'Or if they just didn't like their people,' Michael said. 'Like us with Rhubarb and Valentina.'

'All the stray cats would come,' Em put in, 'and the ones that got washed and combed every day and taken to cat shows.'

'Horses,' Carrie said, 'who had been beaten or starved. Or kicked in the ribs and jerked in the mouth at the same time. Horses would come, from all over the country.'

'From all over England,' Tom said.

'From all over the world!' Michael cried, and Charlie gave a single bark, like laughter.

'They would all come to us here at World's End.' Carrie sat on the stone floor with Perpetua's weary, wounded head in her lap. 'To the end of suffering. The End of the World.'

Ten

That was a dream, but Perpetua was real, with her growing strength, and her flecked white coat growing softer and looser, and the light coming back into her beaten amber eyes.

She was very restless. As soon as she could stand, she wandered round the room, whining and scratching at the door. In the garden, she staggered a few steps, sniffing, then raised her head to howl, before her weak legs collapsed her on to the grass.

And sure enough, when she was strong enough to run, she did go off and tell another dog about World's End. She brought it back with her. A puppy. Her own puppy. They found it in the hay loft, a thin, runty puppy with a blunt speckled head and legs too long for its body.

They called it Moses, after the baby in the Bible who was found in the bulrushes, which was not so different from being found in the hay.

'Call it what you like,' Mr Mismo said. 'It's got fleas.' He had dropped in for a cup of tea, perched up at the high counter of what used to be the public bar, which they now used for a dining-room.

'All puppies have fleas,' Em said.

'What you want to do' – Mr Mismo drank tea out of his saucer, because his wife was waiting for him – 'is to dust that pup with pastry flour. Self-raising, of course.' He was an encyclopedia of weird remedies. Some of them worked. Some of them didn't.

A horn sounded from the lane. Mrs Mismo, who would not get out of the car in her good shopping shoes, was waiting for him to drive her into Town.

That night, with Perpetua and the flea-ridden puppy on the end of her bed, and Charlie under it, to show that he was jealous, Carrie went to the window to call Penny-Come-Quick, and saw a moving light through the gaps in the high door of the hay loft.

She went to wake Tom. 'You imagined it,' he said, 'like you imagined the ghost on the stairs.'

'Come and see. It looks like a torch.'

Grumbling, he went down the passage to her room. The light had gone out. He grumbled back to bed. He had been out on Old Red all day and would be out again early tomorrow, trying to find a job as errand boy, stock boy, cow hand, dish washer, anything. It had been easy to say, 'I'll leave school and get a job.' Not so easy to do it.

Carrie got up early to make him her special breakfast of greasy bacon and flat eggs and burned toast. It was not yet quite light as she stood at the door under the inn sign to wave him Good Luck. It must be her imagination that made her think she saw a face watching her through a gap in the hedge that separated the front grass plot from the stable yard.

'I am going mad,' she thought, like Valentina. 'I really do see things.' Soon she would no longer know what was real and what was imaginary and they would lay her on a couch, like that girl Frenzie at school, and try to talk it out of her.

She bent her knees to look straight into the gap in the

44

hedge. Staring at her, a few yards away, was a boy's brown pointed face like a goblin, with dark, unblinking eyes.

'Wha-what do you want?' Carrie licked her lips. Her mouth was suddenly as dry as a desert, although she had drunk two mugs of last night's stewed-up tea.

The boy butted his head forward and scrabbled himself through the hedge with tough scratched hands.

He was about Carrie's age, perhaps a bit younger

'I want my dogs.' He stood up. He was about Carrie's age, perhaps a bit younger. Skinny, but neat and wiry, not all over the place with huge dangling hands and feet, like Tom.

'What dogs?' She was afraid she knew what he meant, but she shook back her hair and opened her eyes wide, to look innocent.

45

'The pointer and her puppy.'

'She's not really much of a pointer. There's more terrier in her, and perhaps some springer.' Carrie got interested in Perpetua's ancestry, and then remembered. 'She was wounded and starving. We rescued her. Go away, or I'll prosecute you.'

The boy put his hands in his pockets and smiled in a weary sort of way, as if she were a grown-up who had got hold of the wrong end of the stick. '*I* rescued her,' he said patiently. 'When she growled at Bernie because of her puppy, he hit her with a spade – I was spying on him – so I had to get her away. I went back for the puppy later.'

'Who's Bernie?'

'Black Bernie. Black name, black soul. He lives in one of those shacks at the old rubbish pit. Bottle Dump, they call it. He catches stray dogs and cats – sometimes not even strays, but people's pets – and sells them.'

'Who to?'

'A laboratory.'

'What for?'

'To experiment on. They practise operations on them, and inject them with germs.' He picked a stick out of the hedge and broke it in tiny pieces with his thin brown fingers. 'They poison them.'

'How do you know?' Carrie's scalp was prickling with horror.

'I know things. My father works for the Railway. He's seen Black Bernie bring animals to the station in boxes. He says it's for the good of the human race, my father does.'

'That's not *fair*!'

'Especially as it's all the same thing. Dead people come back to life as animals, you know, and animals as people. That cat of mine you stole, the ginger one, I think she may be my great-aunt Gertrude.'

'Her name's Pip. And she's orange, not ginger. We didn't steal her. We found her ages ago, when we first came here.'

'I know.' The boy bent swiftly down to pick a piece of grass to chew. He had a pointed lock of dark hair that fell over one eye. 'I saw you. I'd brought Gertrude here to hide. I'd got into the house.'

'*I saw you.*' Carrie stared at him, remembering the picnic at the top of the meadow, and the face she had thought she saw beside the tattered curtain.

'Yes.' The boy nodded. 'I thought you did.'

'Why didn't you come and tell us about Pip when we moved in? Why didn't you tell us about Perpetua and her puppy instead of trying to hide them?'

'I thought you'd tell.'

'Tell? I'll *help* you! What's your name?'

'Lester. I don't like it. In my last life, I was called Rajah.'

'Why?'

'I was a circus elephant. They beat me, so I stampeded and they shot me.'

'How do you know?'

'What's your name?' he asked, instead of answering.

'Carrie.'

'How do *you* know?'

'Well, I – I remember.'

'That's it.'

He remembered being an elephant! Carrie stared at him. He had dark shining eyes, like washed grapes, and a gleeful goblin smile. He used his hands like birds' wings when he talked, and made sudden, darting movements, casting himself on the ground and rolling over, jumping up and running in a small circle leaning inwards, as if he had more energy in him than he could stand.

'Don't you remember who you were?' he asked.

'No. I mean . . .' She didn't want to disappoint this extraordinary boy. 'I expect I was a horse. I often feel like one.'

'Black Bernie's got a horse at Bottle Dump. It's thin and miserable. It eats the wood off the shed where he keeps it, because it's starving.'

'Why don't you tell the police?'

'And be pinched for stealing his cats and dogs?'

'Could we buy the horse?' She could see it so clearly, almost feel it and smell it, see herself leading it away from

47

the prison of Bottle Dump, thin and lame and needing her.

'What with?'

'I might be able to get the money.' *Dear Uncle Rudolf, I am writing to ask if you could possibly lend me some money for something terribly important* . . . 'Go and ask Black Bernie how much he'd sell it for.'

'I can't,' Lester said. 'He knows me. I was scouting round, looking for the puppy, and he came out with a gun and yelled, "If I ever see you round here again, I'll blow your head off!" '

'But I could go.' Carrie was in a fever of excitement. The day had looked dreary. Getting up in the dark, ruining poor Tom's breakfast, seeing him ride off so forlorn with Old Red going 'Squee-clunk' as the pedal hit the chain guard. Now it was beginning to look marvellous.

'Come on then!' Lester ran into the lane, looked quickly right and left for spies, and was off into the wood with his arms spread wide. 'If you think you're flying,' he called back, 'you are!'

Carrie raced after him. It was only afterwards, remembering, that she thought they really *had* flown through the green tunnel of the beech trees. Had they? With Lester you never knew. He was extraordinary. The most extraordinary boy she had ever met.

Eleven

He led her across fields she had never seen, over hidden ditches like elephant traps, through secret gaps in thick thorn hedges and down winding car tracks she never knew existed. With Lester, you had the feeling that he had invented, not only the adventure, but a whole new landscape.

They came at last to Bottle Dump, an old gravel quarry, long disused, with hillocks of disgusting rubbish and a few old cars upside down without glass or wheels.

Lester pulled Carrie behind a bush and pointed to the steep cliff at the far end of the pit. 'That's where they still see the Headless Horseman, galloping to his death.' He made a dash with her to another bush from where they could see into the quarry. 'And that's where Bernie lives, rot his black soul.'

Some dilapidated shacks made of old boards and beaten-out tin cans leaned drunkenly against each other. Outside, tied on a short chain to a piece of rusted iron, a thin brown horse with a mangy tail and big bony knees nosed hopelessly among old newspapers and rotting cabbage stalks.

'Oh, Lester—' Carrie looked round, but he had disappeared as if he had never been there. She walked forward. The horse raised his head and backed away as far as the chain would go. What had Black Bernie done to make him so terrified of people?

'Come on, boy. It's all right.' She walked towards him with her hand out. The horse stood quivering, ears tight back, sweat already darkening the stringy neck.

Carrie knew how animals talked and got to know each other. She put her hands behind her back and stuck her head forward and blew gently down her nose. The horse squared his nostrils. One ear came cautiously forward. She sent her breath towards him like a message, coming closer. To her joy, the other ear swung forward and he blew back at her. The chain grew slack. He relaxed, dropped his head, and they stood with their faces together, blowing and making friends, until there was a hideous yell from one of the shacks, and Carrie and the horse shied apart in terror.

Black Bernie looked as evil as his name. He had filthy tangled hair and beard, clothes stiff with dirt and grease, one yellow eye squinting at Carrie along the barrel of a huge gun like a blunderbuss.

'Get out of here!' He stepped through the doorway. Carrie would have turned and run, but since Lester was watching her from some hiding-place, she had to make herself step forward.

'I came to see if you would sell your horse.'

49

Black Bernie looked as evil as his name

'That ugly brute?' Black Bernie raised his head, but kept the gun to his shoulder.

'He's beautiful. Just what I want.'

'Then you must be a worse fool than you look. Get out! I'm sick of you rotten kids hanging round here.'

He turned to go inside, putting down his gun, and Carrie ran forward before he shut the door. 'I really want to buy him. How—'

'Get out, I said!' Black Bernie held the door almost shut and stuck his horrid tangled head through the gap. Beyond, Carrie got a glimpse of the filthy inside of the shack, where something was cooking that smelled like putrid cod heads.

'How much?'

'One hundred pounds.' He laughed, showing black and rotted teeth in the cave of his mouth.

'A hundred pounds!' She'd be lucky to get a hundred *pennies* out of the Prince of Plumbers, who had already cut down their allowance. That was why Tom *had* to find a job.

'Anyway,' jeered Black Bernie, closing one yellow eye and putting a warty finger to the side of his purple nose, 'it's too late. I'm sending him to the coast tomorrow with One-Eyed Jake, the Pig Man, to ship to Belgium. Brute's worth more dead than alive. They like horse meat over there.' He threw back his head in a laugh like sulphur fumes and slammed the door.

Carrie could not bear to look at the horse again. She stumbled out of Bottle Dump, tripping and cursing and sobbing, and ran down the rutted track, away from that terrible place.

'Zo,' said a voice behind her. 'Zo, now vee make a plan, yah?'

Half blind with tears, she turned to see Lester following her at a sprightly trot.

'What plan?'

'Listen.' With one of his sudden movements, he pulled her down on to the grass under the hedge and began to talk fast. 'Listen . . .'

'Now listen,' they said to Michael. 'Listen very carefully. You've got to do exactly what we tell you.'

It was that evening. Carrie had not told Michael about the Plan until she got him away from the house, through the beech wood and down the path to the crossroads where Lester waited in a hollow tree, playing the mouth organ as softly and sadly as the wind on an autumn night.

She had not told anyone about the Plan. Em might have said, 'Yes, that's all right, *but* ...' and pointed out all the snags. Tom, who was tired and grouchy after a long hopeless day of job hunting, might have played Man of the House and said, 'I won't let you do it. It's against the Law.'

Michael only said, when they had told him the Plan and his part in it, 'That's easy. I thought you said it was going to be dangerous and difficult.'

When Lester hopped out of the hollow tree, putting his mouth organ in his pocket, Carrie said politely, 'This is my brother, Michael.'

They said 'Hullo' without looking at each other, the way boys did. Then Lester turned swiftly, bent at the knees and put his face close to Michael's. 'Can I trust you?'

Michael was unmoved. 'Everybody else does,' he said calmly.

'Good.'

Carrie could see that Lester liked him, although he was little. When they had decided they needed a third person, and she had said, 'There's my brother, but he's very young,' Lester had said, 'Age is only a stupid label. He might be thousands of years old, for all you know. He might be a re-incarnated dinosaur.'

'Are you prepared,' he asked Michael, 'for a mission fraught with peril and hardship?'

'Well, I'm ready for a bit of a change from cleaning out the chicken house, if that's what you mean.'

The Plan was this:

The road down which One-Eyed Jake, the Pig Man, must drive his van from Bottle Dump to the main road to the coast had recently been under repair. A lorry had skidded through one side of a narrow bridge – 'No harm done, shallow water, the driver climbed out with the wireless still playing. I was first on the scene,' said Lester, who didn't seem to miss a thing.

While the bridge was being repaired, a detour sign had been set up at this crossroads to send traffic round in a loop through the village of Wareham, and back on to the road on the other side of the bridge.

After the repairs were finished, the detour sign was taken down, but not away. It was lying in the ditch, a board with legs. 'DETOUR THROUGH WAREHAM.'

They took Michael over to see it. 'DOCTOR THROW WAR HAM,' he read. 'What on earth does that mean?'

'What's the matter with this boy?' Lester asked, not crossly, but curiously. 'Can't he read?'

'Of course he can,' Carrie said. 'He just reads differently.'

'I don't blame him,' Lester said. 'Everyone does everything the same these days, like sheep.'

'Henry doesn't,' Michael began. 'He never—' But Lester told him to cut out the social chatter and listen to orders.

Tomorrow was Sunday. One-Eyed Jake, said Lester, who knew everything about everybody in this neighbourhood, including people who probably did not exist, drove his wife to chapel in the morning. He could not get to Bottle Dump before two, which meant that after pushing or pulling the brown horse into his smelly pig van, he would pass this crossroads some time after two-thirty.

Michael would wait hidden in the hollow tree. As soon as the van went through he would nip out and set up the detour sign behind it in the road, so that other cars would go off through Wareham and not see what was up.

'What will be up?'

'Carrie and I. Except she'll be down. She'll be lying in the road. Old One-Eye will stop and get out to see if she's dead. I'll open the tail gate of the van, grab the horse, shut the gate and away with him through the hedge and into the field while your sister is screaming her silly head off to cover the noise. Perfect, eh?'

Telling the beautiful Plan, he had begun to jump about in

53

the road, acting it out, casting himself down, toddling and peering like One-Eyed Jake, opening an imaginary tail gate and pulling on an invisible halter rope.

Michael folded his arms. 'All but one thing,' he said. 'What about cars coming the other way?'

'I told you he was clever,' Carrie said. 'At our last school they called him stupid, because he spells his name differently every time.'

'He's a genius,' Lester said. 'But so am I. We're going to put up a detour sign on the other side of the bridge, at the side of the road so that Jake will drive on past it and off to the docks with his empty van. They've taken away that sign, but my friend Garroway, who's a sign painter, is making me another. I told him it was for a play. "All this play-acting," he said. "It's not right on a Sunday." So I said it was for a noble cause, which it is.'

'Noble.' Carrie thought about the poor thin brown horse, so very different from Penny-Come-Quick and all the marvellous horses she had imagined bringing home to her white-washed stable under the thatch. But he was noble too, because he was a horse.

Before they went home, Lester said to Carrie and Michael, 'You swear you won't tell?'

'We swear.'

'But you must swear on blood.'

Out of his pocket – it was surprising how he managed to look so thin and neat and yet carry on him thousands of essential things like chocolate, a screwdriver, putty, the mouth organ – he produced a small hairbrush. They each banged the back of their hands with the bristles, then whirled their arms round and round like windmills until pricks of blood started up. Then they pressed the backs of their hands together to mingle the blood, shut their eyes and groaned, deep in their throats. 'I swear.'

When Carrie opened her eyes, Lester was gone. She licked the blood off the back of her hand. Michael wiped his in his hair. As they went down the road to World's End, they heard, far away across a hay field, a few curly notes of the mouth organ, like squiggles on the air.

54

Twelve

On Sunday, they were so excited, they could hardly get through the morning. Michael was so careful not to break the blood oath that he hardly breathed. When Tom asked him at breakfast, 'What are you going to do today?' Carrie thought he would burst, sitting up at the high counter, looking at himself in the glass behind the bar with his mouth tight shut and his eyes popping out above his puffed red cheeks.

'What's the matter? Has he got the mumps?' None of them had been ill since they had been at World's End, although Valentina's friend Rose Arbuckle had predicted with gloomy glee that they would all get chesty. They did not want ever to have to go to a doctor, in case he told their mother they should not live alone.

'He's allergic to sour milk,' Carrie said.

'Then he should learn to put it on the stone slab in the larder and not leave it by the stove.'

'I did.' Michael let out his breath. 'And Pip got at it.'

Nobody said, as they would have at Aunt Valentina's or in almost any other household, 'Drat that thieving cat.' Pip was going to be a mother. She needed the milk.

'What are *you* going to do, Carrie?'

'I might go for a walk this afternoon.' She swung her long hair forward, because her face was getting red.

'I'll come with you,' Em said. Usually she hated walks.

'Oh. Well – look, you don't have to.'

'Don't think I want to.' Em fired up. 'I was only being kind.'

'I'd rather go by myself,' Carrie mumbled.

'Why?' Em lifted one side of Carrie's hair and put her high-cheeked kitten face close, to see what she was up to.

'I want to make up poetry.' Carrie could not look at her.

'Oh spare us. Oh excuse *me*.' Em climbed off the stool and clumped out of the room in Wellington boots, thumping her feet like a drum horse. 'I'm sorry I bothered your genius.'

Carrie and Michael were going to slip away at one-thirty. The whole morning pointed to that hour. The only watch in the family, which was hung on a nail in the kitchen because they had no clock, dragged as if time were running down to a standstill.

Eleven-thirty. Eleven-forty-five. Not long now. The hands of the watch went faster, and then at eleven-fifty-four as Carrie passed through the kitchen to check one more time, sounds of disaster came from the lane.

A horn. Crunch of tyres on gravel. Voices. 'Hullo, there! Anyone at home?' Uncle Rudolf.

'Yoo-hoo, children! Here we are!' Valentina.

'Oh! My ankle's turned. Oh come and help me!' Rot and darn it. Rose Arbuckle.

Torture! Had they come for lunch? Carrie did not dare to ask. She went out, dragging her feet. Valentina kissed her and said how thin she was, and that she would get lockjaw if she didn't wear shoes. Uncle Rudolf waved his walking stick at Perpetua's puppy Moses, who came through the hedge from the stable yard in joyous welcome. Rose Arbuckle tottered up the millstone path, leaning heavily on Carrie's shoulder, her long cold fingers pinching.

All the other children had disappeared – the rats! – so Carrie took the grown-ups inside and showed them round the ground floor. Not upstairs, because the beds were hardly ever made, and certainly not on Sunday, which was a day of rest from menial work.

The sitting-room, which had once been the lounge of the inn, was quite cosy, with some deck chairs they had found in the barn and an old velvet curtain over a trunk for a sofa, and the Clydesdale horseshoes tacked up round the fireplace. But Valentina looked round and said, 'Isn't there somewhere we can sit down?'

Carrie took them into the kitchen. Two of the cats were on the table, finishing up someone's breakfast kippers. The sink was full of plates and cups, because they didn't wash up until there was nothing left to use. A line of torn clothes, not much cleaner than before they were washed, hung across one corner of the ceiling, because Em thought it looked like rain.

'My dear,' Val said, not unhappily. 'It's a slum.'

'Come into the dining-room. I'll make some tea,' Carrie heard herself saying, although she did not want to do anything that would make them stay. The watch on the nail already said after half past twelve.

She was proud of the dining-room, with its polished mahogany bar, and its old pictures of Spanish ladies drinking glasses of port, and merry huntsmen with tankards, but Rose Arbuckle cried in the doorway, 'My sakes! It looks like a public bar,' and drew back, treading on Carrie's bare toes with her sharp London heel.

She was finally persuaded that there was nothing to fear. Carrie got them on to the high stools at the bar – 'Oh, my poor ankle!' – and dashed to put on the kettle and call the others.

Em was very polite. 'Won't you stay for lunch?' She wanted to show off that she could cook. Carrie could have killed her. If they didn't leave soon, she and Michael would never get away in time. One-Eyed Jake's van would come through before they got there and the whole plan would be wrecked, the horse doomed, and Lester would never speak to her again.

'No, we just stopped in on our way to lunch with some friends across the river,' Uncle Rudolf said. Carrie and Michael let out their breath on sighs of relief.

'That boy sounds wheezy,' Valentina said. 'Are you sure you're all right here on your own?' Her painted face was twisted with the struggle between feeling she ought to say, 'You must come back with us,' and dreading they might say, 'Yes.'

'Everything's fine,' Tom said, very heartily, kicking a dirty plate under a chair and going to the door to shake his fist at Henry the ram, who was butting against it from outside, wanting to join the party.

Rose Arbuckle sat and stared at herself glumly in the carved, gold-framed mirror behind the bar, though why she should want to look at herself when she looked like that, no one knew.

Would they never go? Carrie could see Uncle Rudolf's watch. His hand lay on the counter while he told a long and boring story about a strike at the plumbing factory. Money was tight. That was why he had had to cut down their allowance, although Carrie noticed that he had a new Princely pearl in his tiepin and that Valentina had a large new ring which might be a fake but was more likely to be a diamond.

'Well,' she managed to say when he paused to think of a word bad enough to describe the strikers who wanted more money, 'if you'll excuse me, it's time I—'

Tom frowned at her and shook his head, thinking she was only going for a walk to make up poetry.

Michael tried. 'If you want to get to Beddington before two, Uncle Rhubarb, it's quite a long way.'

'Nonsense, it's only just across the river.'

'There's been a flood,' Michael invented, although there had been no rain for a week. 'That bridge might be closed, and you'd have to cross much farther down, Uncle Rhubarb.'

'Don't call me that.' But they began to go at last. Michael went out to hold Henry, and they went down the path, agonizingly slow, going back for gloves, for a handbag, for Uncle Rudolf's walking stick, while Carrie bustled behind them like a sheepdog, almost barking to get them into the car. It was after one-fifteen.

Maddeningly, Valentina stopped to show Uncle Rudolf a tall weed (there were no flowers). 'Isn't that Deadly Nightshade, dear?'

Rose Arbuckle side-stepped the weed with a faint scream. She was almost at the car when Henry, who loved new people, tore himself loose from Michael and bounded at her over the grass with his wool wobbling like a fat lady.

She made a dash for the car, tore open the back door and got in. But Henry was right behind her, shoving, and before she could shut the door, he had pushed in with her. Tom and Carrie and Em and Michael doubled up with laughter as the door on the opposite side flew open, and Rose Arbuckle fell out, with all her scarves flying, and Henry after her.

Surprisingly agile for one so frail she jumped on to the bonnet of the car with her feet drawn up, screaming loud enough to be heard by all the people in the village who had not yet fallen asleep in front of the television.

Henry leaned thoughtfully against the front wheel and stared at her with love.

'Help!' cried Rose Arbuckle. 'Save me!'

'You're scratching my paint,' Uncle Rudolf said.

When Michael took Henry away, Rose Arbuckle wanted to go back into the house for a lie-down to calm her nerves, but Carrie brushed her down and jollied her along and steered her into the car. She somehow got the others in, and stood back and began to wave even before Uncle Rudolf had started the engine.

At last they were gone.

'You were a bit rude, Carrie,' Tom said. 'Rushing them off like that.'

'Sorry! Sorry!' Carrie stood on tiptoe like a diver, took a deep breath and then ran. Round to the back of the house to meet Michael limping round from the other side, across the bottom of the meadow, into the wood, twisting among the great cool trees, and out on to the road out of sight of the house, running, running – why couldn't she fly this time? – for the crossroads.

Thirteen

No sign of Lester. He hadn't come! Or he was disgusted with them for being five minutes late, and had gone away.

'What can we do?' Could Michael set up the detour sign behind Jake's van and then run the half-mile down the road in time to pull the horse out of the van while Jake was still stopped, looking at Carrie's body? Could Carrie do that while Michael lay in the road? Impossible. They could not do it without Lester.

Carrie sat down on a heap of stones with her head in her hands. Michael began to walk home, exaggerating his limp.

The dry grass and twigs in the ditch stirred and heaved and became Lester, jumping up like a grinning jack-in-the-box.

'Just trying out my camouflage,' he said. 'Come back, young Mike!'

Michael came back, limping less. 'I knew you were there all the time.'

Carrie and Lester left him in the hollow tree and ran off down the road towards the bridge. They did not talk. They knew what they had to do. They stopped at the agreed place, just before the bridge, and Lester took a bottle of tomato ketchup out of his pocket.

'Blood,' he said.

'That's overdoing it.'

'Just a little.' Lester wanted blood. Carrie let him put a smear of ketchup on her chin and some up in the edge of her hair. 'Hit in the head, you see. That's why you blacked out.'

One or two cars came by. Carrie and Lester whistled and threw stones into the stream, as if they were just out for a walk. A boy and a girl pedalled towards them on a tandem bicycle, maddeningly slow, enjoying the scenery. If the van was close behind, it would catch up with them and they would see everything.

At the foot of the hump-backed bridge, the boy got off.

'*Lovers*,' said Lester bitterly. Were they going to lean moonily over the edge of the bridge?

He made the sign of the evil eye at them with his fingers. But the boy had only got off to push the bicycle up the hump because the girl was heavy, with a rear view like a hay stack, toppling on the overloaded bicycle.

They were gone. Down the road in the distance came

slowly . . . a car . . . or a van. Lester clutched Carrie's arm and hissed, *'That's it!'*

He jumped into the ditch and burrowed under the grass and leaves he had collected. Carrie lay down in the road. She must not move. What if One-Eyed Jake's one eye was so dim that he drove straight on over her? There would be more than ketchup on her face then.

The road began to vibrate slightly beneath her. With her eyes shut, she heard the engine, far away, coming nearer and nearer. Very near. The rattle and roar were right on top of her. She was just going to jump up and run, when there was a squeal of brakes and the van stopped. It must be a very old van. It panted slightly and let out a hiss like a steam engine.

There was another squealing too, which did not stop. One-Eyed Jake the Pig Man had some pigs in there as well as a horse. Were they going to Belgium too?

'Hullo, hullo, what's all this then?' A smell of stale tobacco, beer, garlic – Jake bending over her, and she groaned without opening her eyes.

'If you're alive,' he said, in a wheezy voice that sounded like the bellows of the harmonium in the village church, 'get up out of the road and let me by.'

'Oh – oh my back!' Just about now, Lester would be letting down the tail gate. Carrie began to scream and blubber, rolling about and making as much noise as she could. Recognizing a fellow-squealer, the pigs in the van set up as much racket as if Lester were a butcher with a knife, instead of a boy with a mission.

Between Carrie and the pigs, the noise was enough to drown the sound of ten horses clattering out of the van. Everything was going even better than planned. If only Michael had done his job . . . if only a car did not come by . . .

'Come on now, girl.' Jake stirred Carrie with his boot. Was he going to kick her over to the side of the road? She had to open her eyes and look at him. What she saw made her close them again quickly and roll over with her face in the road, still wailing.

61

She had expected somebody ugly. Anyone who would drive a horse to the slaughterhouse could not look like Prince Charming. She had expected an eyepatch, or a closed-up eye. What she had not thought of was a huge red beard bristling up into whiskers all round a face peppered with freckles until it became a thatch of wild flaming hair.

One eye was a small green pebble. The other was almost as big as a ping-pong ball, green and yellow like a marble. Which was real and which was glass? They both stared in different directions.

'I don't believe you're hurt at all,' Jake wheezed suspiciously.

'I am.' She sat up. 'A car knocked me down. Hit and run.' She remembered she was supposed to be hurt and added, 'Oh my back!'

'I'll take you to the hospital.' One-Eyed Jake held out a large freckled hand with a big ring on one finger, made of bent horseshoe nails. He pulled her hard. If she *had* hurt her back, it would have finished her.

She sat up quickly and said, 'It's clicked back. It's better.' She had heard the noise of the tail gate being shut. 'Oh, thank you, thank you. Oh, you're so kind.'

She began to gabble loudly, to cover any noise of hooves before Lester got the horse out of sight behind the hedge. 'I'm all right now.' She stood up. Jake got up off his dusty knees. Framed by his fiery red hair and whiskers, his freckled face was grinning with delight, his eyes staring sideways like a chicken. He felt he had done a good deed.

Well, hooray. It was better to make him happy than angry – at least until he got to the docks and found out that his cargo was short of one horse.

'Sure you're all right?' he wheezed. He had a cigarette stub between his lips which didn't seem to get shorter, just stayed there smouldering and taking away his breath.

'Yes, yes, you go on.' He climbed back into the van, Carrie stepped aside and they parted like old friends, waving and grinning at each other as he drove away, the squealing of the pigs rising to a protest as he bumped them over the narrow bridge, and then fading away down the road.

Fourteen

About a week later, Carrie was wheeling a barrow full of stable bedding when Mr Mismo came into the yard.

'What's this, what's this?' he asked, tipping his small turned-up hat over his broad red face. 'You've never gone and got yourself a horse?'

'I'm cleaning out the goat shed.'

'I wasn't born yesterday, old chump. You think I don't know a barrer load of horse manure when I smell one?'

Carrie set down the barrow. 'Well, as a matter of fact—' She had been dying to show the horse to Mr Mismo, but if the news of the kidnapping – horsenapping – had got out, he might put two and two together. He was, as he said, not born yesterday.

'I said they'd come to you, didn't I?' He gave her a funny look from under the hat. Did he suspect anything?

'As a matter of fact' – Carrie shook her hair and gave him her innocent look – 'my uncle *has* got me a horse. That's what he came to tell me last Sunday.'

'Why didn't you tell me?'

'I wanted to surprise you.' When it was necessary to invent a lie, for safety, or to protect someone – in this case Black Bernie's horse – that didn't count as lying. Necessity was the mother of invention. 'Come and see.'

The brown horse had thrown up his head with his ears back, because he was still afraid of men. But when Carrie went up to him, he dropped his mealy nose into her hand and stood quiet, flicking his ears and rolling back his eye as Mr Mismo went all round him, feeling his skin, running a hand down his legs, with the whistling, hissing sound he made when he groomed Princess Margaret Rose.

When he had finished, all he said was, 'Brown bread. A load of brown bread every three days and a small cigar to chew once a week to clean out his system. And plenty of Doctor Green.'

'We can't afford a vet.'

'Doctor Green.' He waved a hand. 'All that good sweet grass out there.'

'Oh yes. We've got to finish fencing the meadow.' They could not buy rails or posts or even wire, so they were using everything they could find to patch up the hedges and broken-down fence of the meadow that ran up the gentle hillside behind the house. Drainpipes, bits of split planking, a rotting door they found behind the barn, sheltering thousands of wood lice, an iron bedstead that Michael had begged from an old cottage lady and dragged home up the lane.

As Mr Mismo left, he asked casually, 'Where did your uncle get this champion hoss?'

'I – I don't know.' Carrie buried her face in John's wispy mane, which she rubbed every day with oil, to make it grow. She hated not to tell Mr Mismo the truth. She had a feeling he would have enjoyed the story of One-Eyed Jake and the horsenapping. But he was still a grown-up. And it was still horse stealing.

She had told Tom, of course. She had to. He saw Lester and her coming down the lane with the horse, practically carrying him because he was so tired.

'Horse stealing?' he said, and Carrie said, 'As a matter of fact, yes,' and excitedly began to tell him the whole marvellous adventure.

When she had finished, Lester added, 'It was my idea.'

They watched Tom. He looked solemn, his long face, half-boy, half-man considering. Then he let out a shout of laughter and jumped into the air, his hair, which Valentina had tried to get at with the nail scissors from her handbag, flying like a mane.

'I think it was a marvellous idea! Why didn't you let me help?'

'We thought,' said Lester, 'you were old enough to know better.'

'This boy is rude,' Tom said. 'Who is he?'

'I told you. A friend of mine. Lester.'

'Lester who?'

'I don't know.' Lester had not told Carrie his surname, nor where he lived. With Lester, you didn't waste time on that kind of boring question. With Lester, you asked questions like, 'Do you think Mr Mismo's bull might once have been Henry VIII?' and, 'Why do animals want to die alone?'

'I'm incognito,' Lester said mysteriously. 'No man knows my name.'

'Because you're a horse thief?' Tom was grinning.

'Don't ask,' Lester said, and they both laughed.

When they showed the brown horse to Em, she said the same thing as Tom: 'Why didn't you let me help?'

'We will next time,' Lester said. Now he had met all the family, and they all seemed to like each other. Carrie was relieved. It was wretched when you liked someone, and the other people you liked didn't.

'But if I'd been there,' Em said, 'I'd have taken the pigs out of the van too. It's just as bad for them.'

'Pigs are born to be eaten,' Tom said, and Em kicked him in the shin.

'That's a rotten thing to say.'

'You eat bacon and sausages,' Tom said.

'That's different. *That* pig has already been killed. It won't bring it back to life if I don't eat it.'

'But they wouldn't kill another one,' Lester said, 'if you didn't.'

'Or you.' Em stuck out her pointed tongue at him. She could be as rude to people she had just met as if she had known them for years.

'I don't.'

Don't eat bacon or sausages! How could a boy live and grow to be however old he was, without eating bacon, meaty and mellow, so fragrant in the pan? Or without knowing the gush of savoury steam as you put your fork into a sausage and it burst and spread, crusted brown at the ends, packed with delight? No wonder he was so lean and light.

'Could *you* eat your grandmother?'

Lester began to explain his ideas about people coming back to earth as animals, but all Em said was, 'Well, if your grandmother had already been killed for bacon, it wouldn't make any difference to her either,' and went away to boil a piece of ham for supper.

Carrie worried a bit about whether she ought to be a vegetarian too, but she caught Lester one day, coming down from the top of the meadow (he always approached the house from a different direction, because he would not tell her where he lived), eating a cold beef and pickle sandwich, so she stopped worrying.

All the rest of that summer was taken up with John. They had not finished fencing the meadow, so every day, Carrie put a long rope on his halter and lay in the grass with Henry's wedge-shaped head in her lap, and Moses playing with her hair, while John's teeth tore contentedly at the shorter, sweeter turf and Charlie watched them, sighing in the sun.

Gradually, John's neck and hindquarters filled out and his coat was beginning to shine. He might never, as Mr Mismo said, catch the judge's eye, but he was beginning to look like a horse.

'When are you going to get up on him, old chump?'

'Not just yet.'

'Can't you ride? I'll teach you,' said Mr Mismo, who was always ready to teach anybody anything, whether he knew it or not.

'Of course I can ride. I had a friend who had horses, where we used to live.' From what she had seen of Mr Mismo, sitting far back in the saddle on Princess Margaret with his short legs stuck out, she thought she could teach him a couple of things. 'I want to wait till John's quite fit.'

'Scared?'

'Of course not.' She was scared, but not of John. Behind the joy of having him, knowing each night that he would be there in the morning to greet her with his high call like the trumpets of dawn, she was still a little scared that she would be found out. That One-Eyed Jake would find out. That Black Bernie would find out. That John would be taken away from her. If she was already riding him, the breaking of the tie between them would break her heart.

To strengthen his muscles, she took him for long walks. They went up the meadow, through the gate at the top of the hill and down through Mr Mismo's herd of cows to where the wide brook serpentined its way between the willows. With Charlie and Perpetua and Moses going in and out of the water like otters, they walked along the bank to the bridge which took the Beddington road across. On the other side, they followed the path at the edge of the water meadows where once, long ago, she had seen the man on the bay thoroughbred splashing through the silvery wet grass, and Tom had quoted: '*I think I could turn and live with animals . . . I stand and look at them long and long.*'

That had been the beginning of it all.

She met that same man once, trotting up behind her when she had stopped with John to pick watercress in a marshy corner. He said, 'Hullo.' He was young and sunburned.

'I love your horse,' Carrie said, standing to look at the beautiful bay.

'Isn't he fine? I wish he *was* mine. I like yours,' he said in a friendly way.

'Thank you,' she beamed.

'That's nice.' He smiled down at her. 'People always say something like, "Oh, it's not bad," if you admire something. As if it was a sin to be proud.'

Wandering back down the Beddington road, John plodding behind her with his head down, while Carrie dreamed of what he would be, what they would do together, a horn like the bray of a donkey made them both jump sideways.

Rattle and roar, squeal of pigs, squeal of unoiled brakes. One-Eyed Jake pulled up with a jerk and leaned out of the window to wheeze at her.

'Think you own the whole bloomin' road?'

Both eyes were looking at her, the pebble and the ping-pong ball, but neither seemed to recognize her. The day of the horsenapping, she had been wearing a torn pair of jeans with her hair full of grit and ketchup. Today, she was in a pair of Tom's old shorts, tied up with string, her hair plaited back because it was hot, and tied with a broken shoelace.

But John was John, his head down to the grass verge, because, to him, stopping meant snatching a snack.

Carrie stood her ground, expecting a hoarse roar of rage, but all she got was a wheeze of disgust from among the red beard and whiskers. 'Traipsing all over the road with a bloomin' horse! It's the motorist what pays for the upkeep of the road.'

He hadn't recognized John! 'But a horse has right of way, you know. It says so in the Highway Code.' She only meant to give useful information, but she was so relieved that she could not help grinning up at him, and he thought she was joking, and jerked the pig van forward, missing her bare foot by inches.

He didn't recognize John! She watched him disappear down the road in a cloud of dirty exhaust smoke. That meant Black Bernie wouldn't recognize him either. If there was ever any suspicion, he would say, 'That's not my horse', and Carrie would be safe. John was safe. It was safe now to do three things.

The first thing was to tell her mother. She or Tom went every week to the hospital, where their mother was slowly getting stronger and spending longer and longer each day out of the plaster trough in which she still had to lie at night.

From World's End it was a complicated journey of two different buses, with a two-mile walk in the middle, during which Carrie tried to hitch-hike, although she didn't tell Tom, because he didn't tell her whether he hitch-hiked or walked.

'Don't tell about John,' she had told Tom. 'I want to myself.'

'Why don't you then?'

'Give me time,' she had said, during the weeks when she had still been afraid of losing the horse.

'Let me go,' Carrie said this week.

'No, I'll go. I'm not going to bother going after that job at the snack bar. I'm not going to bother looking for work any more. It's hopeless.' Tom was getting very depressed. He had started out believing he was God's gift to all employers, and found out that no one wanted him.

'Perhaps you'll have more chance now that the summer's ending,' Carrie said.

'You told me something like that when it was beginning.'

'Oh well.' If you loved someone, you would say anything to keep them happy. Tom knew that as well as she did.

'Please let me go to see Mother.'

Tom was too depressed to argue. 'All right. You'll be better company than me.'

And I've got *news* for her! All the way in the bus, walking the two miles of road, mostly backwards with her thumb raised, although no cars stopped, Carrie rehearsed how she was going to tell her mother. Tell her the truth, but make her understand. Tell her, because she'd guess anyway, that they had stolen John, but make her see that there was no other way to save his life.

Why had she worried? She had hardly begun her story. 'Well, you see, there is this man called Black Bernie—' had hardly even begun to describe the pitiful state of John, tied to the piece of rusted iron, when tears rushed into her mother's eyes.

She clutched Carrie's hand and said, 'Oh, couldn't you have saved him?'

'I did.' Carrie told her how.

'Why are you crying, Mrs Fielding?' The Staff Nurse who never smiled bustled up, her starched apron crackling like bird shot. 'Look, you're making your poor little daughter cry too. For shame!'

Fifteen

The next thing was to start riding John.

The cracks in his feet were growing out, so Carrie walked him three miles to the forge, where a boy called Dick, with long hair and a transistor radio, was learning to be a blacksmith. He was, of course, a friend of Lester's – Lester knew all the right people – and he had agreed to shoe John for nothing.

'Have us all in the poorhouse.' The old blacksmith, who did not do much these days except complain about the kind of music that came out of the radio, came out of his cottage next to the forge to see what Dick was doing. 'Putting on free shoes for all these dratted kids.'

' 's an interesting case,' Dick said, bending face down with his long hair hanging over John's hind foot in the lap of his leather apron. 'Feet in a bad way. Good experience for me.'

'What say?' Dick had spoken through a mouthful of nails, and the transistor at full blast.

'Good experience for him,' Carrie shouted in the old man's ear. 'Like barbers learning by giving free haircuts.'

'Stuff! The only experience that long-haired fool needs is a kick in the backside from a Suffolk Punch.' The old blacksmith hobbled back indoors, bent and lamed from years of that kind of 'experience'.

Dick did a good job. When it was done, he gave Carrie a leg up and she rode home, John's shoes clopping pleasantly on the road, the view over the hedges from this new height like seeing a whole new land. People rushed by her in cars like boxes, staring ahead, too low to see anything, even if they bothered to look. Carrie felt very sorry for them.

She had no saddle or bridle, so at first she rode John bareback, in a halter with a dog leash clipped to either side for reins.

He behaved quite well, though it seemed he was more used to being driven, since he answered her voice better than her legs and would rather trot than canter, but his backbone was like riding on top of a fence.

Carrie tried putting a cushion between her and his back, but it always slipped out.

'If you were gripping properly,' said Em, who was watching from an upstairs window while Carrie made circles in the one flat corner of the meadow, 'it wouldn't fall out.'

'You come and try then.' Carrie got off and led John

Dick bent down, John's hind foot in the lap of his leather apron

towards the house, bow-legged because she was sore and stiff.

'Not till you get a saddle.' Em could ride, but she was one of those who could take it or leave it, impossible for a horse fool like Carrie to understand.

'Saddles cost money.' It was all they could do to pay for John's feed.

'You've got almost ten pounds saved.' How did she know? The teddy bear was under a loose board in Carrie's bedroom.

'That's for a horse.'

'You've got a horse.'

'I mean, the one I'll buy.' Ever since she could remember, she had been saving for her dream horse. Her dark grey Arab, her shining black thoroughbred, her bright bay with two white socks ... The perfect horse. The horse to end all horses.

John butted her in the back like a goat. Aren't I it?

'Of course.' She stroked his neck, then turned back to look up at Em again. 'I wish I could make some money.'

'I know a lady who wants a baby sitter,' Em said. She quite liked small children, and had taken care of some of them in the village and houses round about while the mothers went to Town or out to dinner.

'Why don't you go?'

'I have once, but I'll let you have the next job, since you need the money more than me.'

'That's awfully nice of you, Emmie.' Carrie tried not to sound surprised, but it was surprising when she and Em were unselfish with each other.

'Oh, I'm like that. It's my nature.' Em took in her head and shut the window.

When Carrie clanked Old Red up the long avenue to the house where Mrs Potter had three small children for her to take care of, she soon found out why Em had been so nice.

Mrs Potter breezed off in her car after giving Carrie only a few vague instructions, the chief of which was, 'Let them do more or less what they like. I don't believe in restricting children.'

72

What they liked! What the three Potter brats liked was sliding down the front stairs on tin trays, throwing stones at the greenhouse, swinging the cat by the tail, chucking food at the pictures on the dining-room walls, and finally locking Carrie in a garden shed.

She got out by climbing on a heap of coal and wriggling through a tiny window. Filthy and dishevelled, her hands and skirt black with coal dust, she was chasing the Potter children round a flower bed, when Mrs Potter drove up the avenue.

Carrie had just caught the youngest. It bit her and she took a swipe at it, missing, because she was blind with rage.

'She hit me!' The child broke away and ran across the flower bed, trampling petunias and zinnias, and hurled itself at its mother, clawing at her dress.

'I dare say you asked for it.' That was one thing about Mrs Potter. She was not strict, but not sentimental either.

'Dear me,' she said, as she saw the wreck of the front hall, where the trays had pushed up rugs and scratched the floor and toppled over a bust of Julius Caesar. 'They seem to have had a lot of fun.'

'We hate her.' The middle child made a face like a toad.

'I dare say she hates you too,' Mrs Potter said amiably. 'I don't suppose she'll come again.'

'Hooray,' said the eldest child.

'But I *must* go to London tomorrow. Would you come, Carrie dear? I'll give you extra money if they actually hurt you.'

Carrie showed her tooth-bruised hand.

'Draw blood, I mean. Please, dear.'

Carrie wanted to say, 'Get someone else to do your dirty work,' but while she was locked in the garden shed, she had seen something. In the far corner, covered with dust and cobwebs, there was a saddle, obviously not used for ages, but it was a good make and the right size.

'You see, I can't get your sister Esmeralda,' Mrs Potter was saying. Em used her full name when she went on jobs, to sound more dignified. 'Little Jocelyn pushed her into the fish

73

pond, and she wasn't very sporting about it, was she, my darling?'

'Esmeralda stinks,' said little Jocelyn.

'So please help me, Carrie. I can't miss my appointment.'

'Well, I might—' Carrie began, and the middle child said, 'Don't bother.'

'I might come tomorrow, but if I didn't take the money, would you—'

'Give it to *me*!' yelled the eldest child. 'I'll baby sit for Carrie. Whack! Whack!' She thumped the dog who was asleep in the sun. 'You bad Carrie baby, you nasty brat.'

'Would you let me have that old saddle that's in the shed?'

'That old rubbish? My dear, I'll be glad if you take it away. I mean,' added Mrs Potter quickly, as Carrie started for the shed, 'if you'll come tomorrow.'

It was worth it. The children gave her such a bad time the next day that Mrs Potter gave her not only the saddle, but an old snaffle bridle that was hanging on a nail.

One of the Potters had stuck a pin in the rear tyre of Old Red, so Carrie wheeled him home with the saddle on the handlebars.

She spent her toothpaste money on a bar of glycerine soap and cleaned the saddle and bridle, leaving them in the kitchen afterwards, as she had always wanted to do. She had always wanted a kitchen where there was a saddle on the back of a chair and at least one bridle on the knob of a cupboard door.

She began to ride John all over the countryside, exploring, getting lost, coming back sometimes after dark, with a luminous glow round the edges of John's home-going ears and Charlie trotting right behind his heels like a coach dog. She taught John things and he taught her. She finally learned how to make him forget his fast cart trot and slip straight into a rolling canter.

'Looks as if he'd got five legs,' Mr Mismo grumbled, but when Carrie got used to him, he was the most comfortable horse she had ever ridden, because he was hers.

'Use your outside leg!' Mr Mismo was standing in the field like a riding master, while Carrie made circles round him.

'I'm training him to my voice.' She pulled back to a jog. 'When I say, "Canter!" he canters.' John cantered.

'I knew a girl did that,' said Mr Mismo, who always knew someone who had done everything. 'And when she was showing at the International, her worst enemy sat by the edge of the ring and said, "Canter" when it was supposed to be Trot. Laugh!' He slapped his knees.

'Look how he can jump.' Carrie hopped John over the two fallen tree trunks by the hedge. Henry and Lucy the goat, who always schooled themselves while she was schooling John, leaped over the trees behind her.

'Look here.' When she came back to Mr Mismo, his face was serious. 'I'm not sure you've not got a natural jumper there, old dear. He uses his back amazing. See this length from croup to hock?' He ran a hand down the back end of John. 'Yes . . . yes . . . I've seen some ugly customers like this that could jump like deer. It's not the looks, see, nor yet the power. It's the way they use it.'

Carrie did not mind him calling John an ugly customer. She was not surprised that he might turn out to be a jumper. John could do anything.

That night, she decided to do the third thing that she had waited for. She decided that John was fit enough to run with her and Penny-Come-Quick up into the sky where the bygone horses grazed on the Elysian star.

She rode Penny, and John galloped beside them with his neck stretched out and his growing mane and tail flying in the night. It was like a flight. The beat of the hooves on the firmament was like the thrust of wings. Carrie clung to Penny's white mane and the cool night air streamed into her smiling face. She would never get old enough to give up this dream!

On the star, John was introduced to several interesting horses. They met a roan mare who had pulled a covered wagon in the California Gold Rush, and a big Cleveland Bay who had carried his master against the guns in the First World War, and a chariot horse, and Queen Victoria's

Highland pony, and the black stallion Bucephalus.

John was asked to tell his story, so Carrie made one up for him, with all the different homes and jobs she thought he might have had, and all the hard times through which he had worked so bravely, to come at last to Black Bernie and Bottle Dump.

'I thought I was doomed. When they bundled me into that pig van, I knew where I was going.' The other horses nodded. All animals know when they are near the end. 'And then,' he told them, 'I was rescued from the very jaws of death itself.'

Carrie twisted her fingers in Penny's mane, looking modestly down, as John told them the story of the Great Rescue.

'Very interesting,' said Bucephalus, almost before he had finished, 'but wait till you hear what happened to *me*.' He had repeated the story dozens of times, but John was a new ear to listen, so he was able to tell once more the stirring tale of the Battle of Cheironeia.

'My rider, Alexander' (he never called him Master), 'still only a boy of eighteen, was in command of all the cavalry. We thundered down from the hill. I can hear the drumbeat of the hooves now. I can see the flash of that sword blade in the morning sun, striking at Alexander. I reared up and trampled the enemy down, but another was upon us from the side. The cold steel of his spear was actually into my neck – see, here's the scar.' He turned his proud black head to one side. 'But Alexander struck him down. We saved each other's lives that day. Yes, my friends,' like all conceited tellers of tales, he often repeated himself. 'We saved each other's lives.'

Sixteen

Pip's kittens were almost due to be born. The delicate little marmalade cat with the bull's eye striped whiskers had a heavy weight to carry about, like a housewife with an overloaded shopping bag.

She began to look for nests. They found her under beds, on a pile of yellowing newspapers in the old bread oven beside the fireplace, on sacks behind the feed bin, and finally in the loft of the barn, where she had hollowed out a place and covered herself with hay, like a sleeping guinea-pig.

When Carrie found her there, the little cat was in great distress. She was crying with a long-drawn-out yowl, her green eyes staring, her mouth drawn back as she panted in a way that would be natural for a dog, but looked frightening in a cat.

Something was wrong. Carrie had seen kittens born. When they lived in the old Army hut, and before that in the red brick house with the boat in the kitchen, even stray cats dropped in to have their babies, since Carrie's mother had a natural attraction for new life.

Carrie did not know what to do. Tom had got a few days' work with the beet harvest. Michael had gone to the crossroads to wait for the travelling fish van, and try to beg some cods' heads and bits of eel for the cats and dogs. Em had gone to a churchyard with Lester to read epitaphs on old graves.

Emmie, who was part cat, might have known what to do. Panting and heaving, Pip stared up at Carrie. I am dying, she said.

'No you're not.' Carrie picked her up and carried her down to the stable. She laid her in the manger while she saddled John, then with the cat inside her shirt, mounted and rode as smoothly as she could down the lane to Mr Mismo.

He was out. Tyre tracks in the mud, but no car.

She turned and rode back past the house, round the corner and into the deep wood where the leafy branches met high overhead, and John's hooves made a thicker, muffled sound as they trotted on.

The vet was four miles away, in the new housing estates. Carrie thought Pip might die before they got there, but at least she was doing something. Better than standing by wringing her hands.

When she came out of the shelter of the wood, it was raining. Riding with one hand, she held her other arm across her shirt and leaned forward to shelter the cat. The rain drove down like pebbles. John put his ears back and shook his head, but he trotted on. Carrie cantered him on the grassy side of the road, walked a little while to rest him, then trotted on again, his feet clopping hollow on the streaming road. His coat was soaked with sweat and rain. Her hair hung like seaweed, in her eyes, in her mouth. Her clothes were plastered to her. Her bare feet clung by the big toe to the stirrups, blue and yellow with cold.

She did not know where the vet was. In pelting rain, she came into the beginning of the streets of new houses. No one about. A man in a car swerved, as John swerved round a deep puddle.

'Look out!' he yelled.

'Where's the vet?'

He stared at her like an idiot and drove on.

'Where's the vet?' There was a man in a sou'wester and oilskins at the petrol station on the corner. He stared too, as if Carrie were the headless horseman. As if he had never seen a soaked girl on a soaking horse with a dying cat inside her shirt.

'Please! Do you know where the vet lives?'

He shook his head. Rain cascaded off the brim of his yellow sou'wester.

'It's an emergency!'

'Oh well.' That seemed to jog his memory. 'Go up to the crossroads. Turn left, turn right, go past the school. You'll see a sign.'

Carrie clattered away down the hard black roads, turned left, turned right, passed the new school, all glass windows like a hot-house for forcing children's brains, charged up the path at the side of the vet's house, got off and pounded on the door.

Nobody came. She banged the horseshoe knocker, then rang the bell beside a board which said: 'Surgery Hours: 9–11 and 4.30–6.30.'

At last a man in old clothes spattered with paint, and a brush in one hand, opened the door.

'Surgery's not till four-thirty,' he said.

'M-my c-cat is dying.' Carrie's teeth were chattering so with cold and wet and crisis that she could hardly speak.

'Come inside.' The man was quite young, with a smooth tanned face and a mouth ready to curve into a smile. Too young to be a vet. It must be his son. It was – it was the man who rode the bay thoroughbred in the water meadows. She had not recognized him at first without his cap.

'I know you, don't I?' His smile spread, as he remembered too, looking at John. 'Come on in.'

'My horse—'

'There's a shed at the back, behind the kennels. You can put him in there. Here, give puss to me.'

Carrie handed over the damp body, struggling with the life of the kittens inside. She went past a row of kennels with dog runs, put John in the shed, and ran back to the house.

As she went into the waiting-room, the young man came in through the inner door, wearing a white apron over his painting clothes.

'Oh,' Carrie said. 'Are you the vet?'

'Yes. Alec Harvey. It's my first practice. Do you trust me? I want to operate at once. A Caesarian. She may be all right.'

A Caesarian operation meant the way Julius Caesar was born, by cutting open his mother. 'You'll have to help me with the ether,' Alec Harvey said. 'I've no one else here.'

Still shivering from the cold rain, Carrie held the bottle and dropped ether, as he told her, on to the gauze pad over Pip's face of a miniature lion. Her hand was shaking so

79

much that the ether went all over the place and made her feel extraordinarily dizzy.

'Hold on,' said the vet, 'or you'll have the three of us out for the count.'

He shaved the hair from Pip's stomach, and swabbed it with antiseptic. Carrie was afraid at first and wouldn't look. Then Mr Harvey said, 'Look, here's the first kitten!' and as she watched his hands in rubber gloves working so surely and swiftly, she wasn't afraid at all. The kitten gave a sort of moan, a first feeble try at a miaow. It was the most marvellous thing – like a miracle. Life being taken from life.

'Take it,' the vet said. 'In that towel.'

Carrie held out the towel and he put the tiny wet body into it, and while he was getting out the other kitten, he told her what to do: wipe the nose and mouth, rub gently to dry it and help the breathing, and – the kitten began to cry properly, getting the air its lungs needed.

She put it in a box and worked the same way with the other kitten, until it cried too, and when Pip, neatly stitched, began to stir and wake, she turned her head at once towards the box full of mewing. The vet put her in with her kittens. Blindly, they crawled to find the milk, and Pip began to work them over with her rough tongue.

'She's even starting to purr.' Carrie's voice was shaky. Now that the crisis was over, her knees felt so weak that she had to sit down on the enamel stool.

'People are the only ones who have surgical shock and take weeks to recover,' Alec Harvey said. 'That's why I like being an animal doctor.'

'It was exciting,' Carrie said. She would never forget how she had held the new-born life in her hands, and helped it to cry and breathe.

'Wasn't it?' Alec Harvey grinned. 'I never get over the thrill.'

He would keep Pip and her kittens with him for the night. He gave Carrie some cocoa, and lent her a jersey, which hung on her like a jacket, and she went out to get John.

'I'm afraid I can't pay you,' she said at the door.

Carrie would never forget how she had held the new-born life in her hands

'That's all right.' He thought she meant she had come without money. 'Any time will do.'

The rain was almost over. Halfway home, it stopped and the sun came feebly and damply out. They jogged home, steaming gently, clouds of aromatic smoke rising from John.

'Where on earth have you been?' Tom came into the yard as he heard her ride in.

'Pip's had two kittens. Julius and Caesar. At the vet's.' Carrie was so tired, she fell off into Tom's arms.

Next day, Tom took the bus from the village to the housing estate, with a shopping basket on his arm. In his pocket, he had the only watch in the family, taken down from the nail in the kitchen to offer to the vet instead of payment.

When he came back with the basket full of mewing, he was grinning all over his face.

'What's the joke?' Carrie looked into the basket. Caesar was tortoiseshell, an extra toe on each paw. Julius looked like a grey mole. Pip was smiling.

'Life is a joke.' Tom gave the basket to Em, who had Paul riding her shoulder like a mountain goat, furious about the kittens. 'Guess what?'

'You tell.' Tom looked gayer than Carrie had seen him for weeks.

'I've got a job. I started to tell Mr Harvey we couldn't pay him yet. "Until I find work—" I began to say, but before I could give him the watch, he grabbed my arm so hard I nearly dropped the kittens. "You've found it," he said. "I'm desperate for a boy to help me here."'

Seventeen

Tom caught the early bus every morning, and came back in the evening with marvellous tales of setting bones and pulling teeth and diagnosing the diseases of patients who could not talk about their symptoms. The money wasn't much, but he loved the job, even typing out Alec Harvey's bills with one finger and hosing down the dog runs.

Carrie and Em and Michael also went off every morning. They walked to the school in the next village but one, a low rambling old place on the edge of a cricket field, with scarred-up desks and two doors into the playground which said 'Boys' and 'Girls'; relic of long-ago days when they had to be kept separate.

Every afternoon, Carrie rushed home by the short cut across the fields. She stepped out of her only skirt and into her jeans, and leaving skirt and school books and everything else that had accumulated, like tidal seaweed, on her bedroom floor, ran to the stable to start the real business of the day.

She was training John to jump. Mr Mismo was right. Led by Lucy the goat and followed by Henry, weighted with autumn wool, John was going over barrels and tyres and boxes and bits of old prams that Carrie dragged back from the village dump to make jumps of.

'He's a horse in a million.'

'He's a fiddle-headed, five-legged star-gazer, with no more sense than you,' Mr Mismo said fondly, and gave her an old martingale to make John look at his jumps.

School was . . . school. Neither bad nor good. It wasn't as good as the small friendly school where they went when they lived in the old Army hut, but it wasn't as bad as the shrieking, high-powered school that Uncle Rudolf had sent them to in London, where no sum was less than seven figures wide, and you had to sit in a booth with earphones to learn what they said was French.

Carrie was all right. She didn't care about anything except the English lessons, and for those she had a mad, enthusiastic teacher called Mrs Croker, with grey hair cut round a basin and a way of crying, 'Oh curses! Why must we slog through these dreary textbooks when all the glorious poems are waiting for our delight?'

She recited poetry by the hour, waving her arms about and dribbling at the corners of the mouth, while Carrie dreamed to the enchantment of the words.

> *Hoofs thick beating on the hollow hill . . .*

> *'Is there anybody there?' said the Traveller,*
> *Knocking on the moonlit door!*
> *And his horse in silence champed the grasses*
> *Of the forest's ferny floor . . .*

> *Strong gongs groaning as the guns boom far,*
> *Don John of Austria is going to the war . . .*

It was exciting and soothing at the same time.

Em was all right. She was a person contained within herself. If people teased her, she kept silent, so they could not know whether she minded. If they pushed or punched, she stepped aside, instead of hitting back. She didn't like the feel of people, only of animals.

Michael was not so all right. His teacher, who wore a green knitted dress that showed her bulges fore and aft, did not understand about spelling. She was no good at teaching or keeping order, so she concentrated on unnecessary things like the difference between Because and Becuas, and Michael's mixing up Of and For and From and Off, and spelling his name Micheal.

He worked quite hard, but Miss McDrane took a mark off for every spelling mistake, which gave him less than 0 out of 10. He was down into minus figures.

There was also the problem that if he forgot to shut up Henry, the sociable ram would follow him to the school building and wait outside, cropping the cricket field, until it was time to go home. So of course some bright boy nicknamed Michael 'Mary', and the others took it up.

One day, Miss McDrane, maddened beyond reason by a class who would not keep quiet when she was in the room, and tore it apart if she went out decided to read aloud Michael's composition, titled, 'What I Want For Christmas.'

'Wat i want form crismus. i wold lik a babby gine pig i hope i get a pen nife form mi boter.'

84

It was a perfectly good composition. Any fool could have known what he meant. But Miss McDrane read it scornfully, pronouncing the words wrong as he had written them, while Michael, as he told Carrie afterwards, felt his ears sticking out like beacons, and wished he could go through the floor into the boiler-room, carved-up desk and all.

' "i hop i get a pen nife form mi boter." You see, everyone, Michael has invented a new language.' Miss McDrane laughed. The class laughed with her and chanted:

> *Mary had a little lamb.*
> *Its fleece was grey as mud.*
> *And everywhere that Mary went,*
> *They said he was a dud!'*

Michael leaped from his seat with a yell and began lashing out wildly. Stupid as she was, Miss McDrane realized that she had gone too far. She rushed down the room in her tight knitted dress to stop the fight, and stopped a blow from Michael's fist on the side of her chin.

'Caroline Fielding is wanted in the Head's Office.' A stout girl who ran errands all the time to get out of lessons came into Carrie's geography class.

Carrie jumped up. Mother? was her first thought. As she ran down the long corridor which smelled of shoes and school dinners, she thought, John?

It was only Michael. He was sitting in Mrs Loomis' office sucking a peppermint and kicking the rungs of the chair.

'We've had a spot of trouble with this little boy.' Mrs Loomis talked to Carrie as if she were another grown-up. 'Can you help me to find out what's wrong?'

Carrie knew very well what was wrong. She knew about Miss McDrane, but you didn't complain about teachers to other teachers. You tried to get the better of them by yourself. Not by sneaking.

'I understand your parents—'

'They're away just now,' Carrie said quickly. 'My mother will be home soon.'

'I'd like her to come and have a chat with me.'

Poor mother. She was still so weak that even when she did come home, Mrs Loomis would have to come to her, and probably to her bedroom, if she wanted a chat.

'My brother Tom is head of the house.'

'Perhaps I could talk to him—'

'He's working.' Carrie was not going to tell her about Tom's half day.

Mrs Loomis sighed. 'All right, Michael, you go back to your classroom now, and try to be a gentleman.'

'Yes, Miss Bloomers.'

'Mrs Loomis.'

'Yes,' said Michael, as if that was what he had said.

When he had gone, the headmistress asked Carrie, 'Things are all right, are they, at home?' She fiddled with a paper knife. When she wanted to know something, she asked it casually. When she wanted to say, for instance, 'Who threw that boot through the window of the gym?' she only remarked vaguely in Morning Assembly, 'By the way, people, there's a left boot unclaimed.'

'Marvellous,' Carrie said, and it was true. They were poor as mice and living mostly on baked beans and the flat sticky bread that Em had discovered how to make. But they were together. And they had animals. And an exhausted swallow had dropped in yesterday, as if it was a hotel on his way south. And Tom had cut enough logs from the wood for the fire. And only one room upstairs still let the water in.

'I mean, if you need anything, there are people who can help—'

Mrs Loomis was looking at Carrie's shoes. She stood one foot on top of the other to hide the battered toe, and only succeeded in showing the hole underneath.

'Until your mother comes back, perhaps the Social Worker—'

Miss Nuttishall. 'Come peeking and peering into my cottage as if she had a search warrant,' Carrie had heard one woman tell another in the grocery. No thank you. None of that at World's End.

'Everything's marvellous.' Carrie tried to pull down the

sleeves of the jersey that had fitted her before Em had shrunk it. 'My uncle and aunt are very nice to us. They buy us clothes and food and all that.'

'Very nice,' said Mrs Loomis, looking over her half glasses at the un-get-outable stain on Carrie's only skirt.

And it was almost true. Uncle Rudolf was giving them an allowance, a lot of which went on food for animals, and he and Valentina were trying to be nice, in as much as they had invited all four of them up to London for the weekend.

'Don't let's go,' Em said, when the letter came.

'We must.'

'They think they "must" ask us,' Em said, 'so why can't two Musts make a Needn't?'

They tried to give themselves several excuses. Tom couldn't get away. But Mr Harvey gave him the whole weekend off for good work. They couldn't leave the animals. But Lester was longing to be left in charge of all of them. He was longing to ride John, but he wouldn't when Carrie was there, because she rode better than he did. Michael had nothing to wear. But Mrs Mismo came down the lane with a bag full of things her grandson had grown out of, so Michael was better dressed than anyone.

There was no telephone at World's End. Valentina sent them a telegram: RUDE NOT ANSWER. EXPECTING YOU.

A boy called Arthur brought it out from the village on a fleet post office bicycle.

'It says, "Rude not to answer",' he said, although the telegram was in a sealed envelope. The old lady at the post office, who read all the postcards and steamed open interesting-looking letters, knew everybody's business and passed it on. 'So answer me this,' Arthur went on. 'What is white, has raisins and is terribly dangerous?'

'A shark-infested rice pudding.' Emmie stuck out her tongue and slammed the door.

The weekend was as boring as they had expected. And it reminded them of one or two things that they had got used to doing without.

Hot baths.

At World's End, there was a tin bath hanging on the wall

in the scullery. It was used for many things. Shampooing dogs. Mixing potting soil for the hyacinth bulbs which one of Em's baby-sitting mothers had given her. Storing dirty clothes until someone felt like washing them or putting them on again still dirty. When it was not in use, and when there was enough hot water, the bath was put in front of the sitting-room fire and they took turns in it.

Warmth.

Everyone wore two jerseys at World's End in the winter, in bed and out. To get up in the morning, you had to have the willpower of a crusading saint. It was only John's breakfast neigh, or a dog asking to get out or a cat asking to come in that made you leap from bed to the cold boards and dash down to dress in the kitchen, where they banked up the stove to keep it going all night.

Food.

Roast turkey. Grilled steak. Fruit salad. Chocolate ice. As if to point up the contrast between her life and theirs, Valentina gave them all their favourite kinds of rich and costly food.

'Serve you right if we moved back in,' Tom said with his mouth full at lunch on Sunday.

He was joking, but Valentina's face fell like the blade of the guillotine.

'I've been thinking,' said Uncle Rudolf, catching her fear. 'Perhaps I should give you a bit more money.' They pricked up their ears. Carrie bought an imaginary new bridle. Emmie bought tins of salmon for the cats. Michael bought a pair of rabbits and a bag of barley sugar for Lucy. 'But not,' Uncle Rudolf added, as if he was a mind reader, 'to be spent on that smelly menagerie you keep out there.'

Tom got a bit huffy. Having to take money from him was bad enough. Being told what to do with it was worse. 'I am working, you know,' he said. 'I've got my job.'

Uncle Rudolf pushed out his lips in the shape of 'Pooh', without actually saying it. 'It can't go far, what little you make.'

'It's enough.' Tom snapped his mouth shut in a firm line. His eyes were very angry.

'What for? My dear boy, even my youngest apprentice plumber earns twice what you do.'

The bridle faded, the tinned salmon and the rabbits. If he was going to insult Tom . . .

'No thank you, Uncle Rhubarb.' Michael spoke proudly for them all. 'We can manage prefickly all right.'

Eighteen

Anxious to get away, they left too early for their bus, got on the wrong one, went miles out of their way and got home late. There was no electricity at World's End, but a lamp was lit in a downstairs window. The door opened and animals poured out in a flood of welcome, streaming down the path. Lester was behind them in the doorway, holding a candle which made deep flickering shadows on his goblin face.

He had spent most of his weekend alone at World's End with the animals. He could not have any at home. If his father went within five yards of anything with fur on it, his face swelled up like a streaming tomato.

'Did you ride John?' Carrie asked.

'He bucked.' He did not say whether he had fallen off.

'He never bucks!'

'I think he may have been a cowboy once, out in the Wild West. He's got those kind of knees . . .'

'More likely you put the saddle on too far back,' Em said. She was tired and cross. She looked as if she wanted to cry. Michael could bawl anywhere, and turn it off as suddenly as he turned it on. But Emmie had to go away, up a tree, in the attic, under the raised floor of the woodshed, among the mice and beetles.

It was marvellous to be home. The visit to London and luxury had pointed up the difference between that life and this. The better difference.

What was the point of making a bed if you were going to sleep in it that night? Why brush your hair if you were going out into the wind? Why clean the top of the stove when it was going to get dirty again next time someone fried chips? Why fiddle with a knife and fork when a chicken drumstick tasted better from your fingers? ('Savages,' Aunt Val had moaned at the first meal in London, before they remembered they weren't at home. 'It's taken away my appetite.') Why hurry home from a ride, or from watching squirrels in the wood, or sliding on the frozen duckpond, just because it happened to be the time that ordinary dull people had their tea?

Clothes were the only problem. They had to go to school or go to prison, which even Michael admitted might be worse. But as the winter hardened into icy days, only Michael, in Mrs Mismo's grandson's anorak, had enough to wear.

'Is that the only coat you've got?' Mrs Croker, with a fur hat down over her eyes like a mad trapper, met Carrie outside the school.

'I don't feel the cold.' Carrie hunched the thin jacket round her, keeping her blue hands in the pockets.

' *"That age is best, which is the first, when youth and blood are warmer,"* ' quoted Mrs Croker. 'Isn't there anyone at home with a car?'

'We don't need one. My horse is broken to harness. When I can get the trap mended, we can drive to school in that.'

Tom helped her to mend the floor and the seat of the brown and yellow trap she had found on the day of the picnic. A friend of Lester's, who was a wheelwright, put some new spokes in the wheels. She and Lester got between the shafts and trotted the light trap along to his workshop on the other side of the hill. On the way back, downhill, with the trap trying to go faster than them, Carrie could not feel her feet on the road, and she knew that they were flying.

They stuffed the broken horse collar with Henry's wool. They mended the harness with string and Michael's belt, which didn't keep his trousers up anyway, and added a piece of clothes line to make the broken reins long enough.

Mrs Croker's cousin, who was a baker, lived near the school. He agreed to let Carrie use his stable while his horse and cart were out on the bread rounds. She had been right about John. He put his head into the collar with his eyes shut and his ears back, as if it was very familiar. He backed willingly between the shafts of the trap, stood to be hitched up, and trotted off happily with his ears cocked and his nostrils blowing square, with Carrie and Em and Michael singing behind him on the road to school.

And now, just when they thought it would be winter for ever, it began to get warmer. The animals began to shed their coats. The ground softened. Green daffodil noses grew an inch in a day. Emmie stopped coughing. Carrie's chilblain healed. Michael's nose only ran some of the time. The tortoise put its head out, sighed and took it back in again. The swallow, which had decided to stay here rather than bother to go on south, found another swallow and began to build a mud nest on a rafter of an empty loose box. Perpetua was going to have some more puppies. The kittens, Julius and Caesar, were mad with the spring and with their youth. They sailed from tree to tree like monkeys, and danced on the hill at night, stiff-legged under the moon.

A man from the Society for the Prevention of Cruelty to Animals was going round the neighbourhood, inspecting stables. He found John standing in deep clean straw, with Henry lying on one side of him and Lucy on the other, chewing their cuds. He stayed to lunch (hard-boiled eggs and tinned spaghetti and a jug of cider which he fetched from the Red Lion), and liked everything so much that he gave them a donkey which had run away from a ferocious junk man.

The donkey's name was Leonora. She had a soft grey fringe and dark rings round her beautiful eyes. She had been beaten, but it had not spoiled her nature. She had stuck it out bravely with the junk man, pulling his heavy cart, kicking him when he kicked her, and hoping to be rescued.

One night, she had broken out of her horrid yard among the old iron and rag bags, tried to cross the main highway, been hit by a car and left for dead at the side of the road.

'Heading this way,' Carrie realized. 'The word is getting out, you see. They know they can come here.'

Leonora had only been stunned. She was all right now, except for being blind in one of her beautiful eyes. The white cat roosted on her back like a pigeon, and one of the swallows laid some eggs in the nest above her.

'No such thing as one horse,' Mr Mismo had said. And a donkey was almost a horse. And the Cruelty Man knew of a pony that might want a good home . . .

Everything was wonderful.

Until one day when they drove home from school and found Lester waiting for them, perched on the roof of the hen house, trying to talk some intelligence into the dim brains of Diane and Currier.

He went to a different school, somewhere in the other direction – Carrie still didn't know where he lived – but he knew things that were going on in their school, even things they didn't know themselves.

'It's trouble.' He slid off the hen house roof and they all went into the kitchen and ate bread and jam like starving refugees, standing up with their coats on. They had not had butter, nor even margarine, since they were in London.

One of Lester's many friends was Mrs Croker's cousin, the baker. When his errand boy had taken the day off to have his tonsils out, Lester had taken a day off school to help with the bread round. Carrying the big baskets of loaves to the school on the edge of the cricket field, he had 'happened' to wander down the wrong corridor on his way out, and had overheard a startling conversation.

'They're worried about you,' Lester said. 'It looks like a case of neglect.'

'Oh, rot.'

'Not rot,' Lester said. 'You'll be lucky if it's only the Cruelty to Animals man that comes. They'll send the Cruelty to Children man next, you'll see. That woman is out for blood.'

'What woman?'

'I heard her. I was right there, outside the door.'

'Was it a green door with a stupid-looking knocker made

of *See No Evil, Speak No Evil, Hear No Evil*?' Carrie asked.

'None other.'

Mrs Loomis' door! No one but Lester could crouch with two empty bread baskets outside the Head Mistress' office and not get caught.

' "It is our duty to investigate," she said. "I think I should send over Miss Nuttishall." '

'Miss Nutshell,' Michael said. 'That's torn it.'

Carrie glanced round the room, where dogs and cats lay all over the floor like mats. Everywhere she looked, even just in the kitchen, there was something for a Social Worker to object to. 'When's she coming?'

'Soon, I think. But I saw a figure moving towards the keyhole and I had to vanish.'

Tom came home. They told him. 'Could they make us leave here?'

'They might.'

'I wish Mother was here!' Michael's nose began to run. He was the one who missed his mother the most.

'I wish Dad was,' Em said. She was the one who missed her father the most.

'Well, they're not,' Tom said, irritable because he was worried. 'So we'd better start cleaning this place up.'

'I like it the way it is.'

'*She* won't.'

So now they had to look at the comfortable mess of their beloved home with the eyes of the Dreaded Nutshell. Books on the floor. Clothes hanging on the picture frames. Carrie's saddle on the back of a chair. Old Red's bicycle chain oiling in a vegetable dish. Michael's pebble collection laid out in a maze on the bar. Ants drilling on the pantry shelves. Everything smelling slightly of dog, thick with white hairs, the underneath of the best chair pulled out by the kittens, who had made a nest in the springs inside.

Now they had to see that Miss Nuttishall would see the mounds of fluff under the beds, the mud tracks from the doors, the cobwebs. They saw that the windows were so dirty that you could hardly see out.

So what? They were out of doors most of the time

anyway. But Miss Nuttishall would not see the daffodils and the primroses in the thicket at the edge of the wood, nor the fresh-painted trap with yellow lines like gold thread on its wheels, nor the clean stables where John and Leonora blew sweet hay breath. The Dreaded Nutshell would be too busy poking her disapproving nose through the mess indoors.

'We can never get it cleaned up in time! What are we going to do?'

They looked at each other. No one knew.

Except Lester. 'I have an idea.' He closed one eye.

'Honestly?'

'The day I'm out of ideas,' he said, 'prepare for the end of the world.'

Nineteen

Lester's mother worked 'for an organization'. He wouldn't say what or where. He made it sound as mysterious as a spy ring.

But whatever it was his mother did, she had the weekend off from doing it, and she would come to World's End and help them get it presentable for the eyes of the Dreaded Nutshell.

Lester brought her on Saturday morning, in a little black car like a beetle, with a plastic flower on top of the wireless aerial. She didn't look a bit like a spy. When she struggled herself out of the tight fit of the car, she was a plump, pink-cheeked lady in a flowered overall, with a lot of soft brown hair shedding hairpins all over the place.

'What shall I call her?' Carrie whispered, as she and Lester followed her into the house. 'I don't even know your name.'

She had thought it would be something dashing, like Wildeblood or Fitz-Percy, but Lester said, 'Figg. You can call her Mrs Figg.'

'Is that your name?'

'Why not?'

'Why didn't you tell me?'

'You never asked.'

The sun shone that weekend, but they all worked with Lester's mother inside the house.

'Can't I even ride?' Carrie took a quick breather on the bench outside the front door, eating the marvellous sandwich that Mrs Figg had brought.

'Work first, then play,' Tom said like a grown-up. He was on a ladder, washing the outside of the windows.

'Riding is work. John needs to exercise.'

'Turn him out.' They had finished the fence of the meadow at last. John pushed a bit of it down almost every day, but he never went farther than round to the front of the house to eat the grass there and stare in at the windows.

On Sunday it was Tom's turn to go to the hospital. The ground floor was finished, and Lester's mother said she could do the upstairs by herself.

'All you kids ... getting in my way.' She pretended to grumble, shaking her mop at a cat, swishing her broom round the cobwebs that hung like grey curtains in the corners. 'Get away, you dirty thing!' She poked at a big round spider who sat in the middle of a perfect web he had built between a shelf and the top of a cupboard.

'He's only doing his job,' Lester said. 'Leave him alone.'

'Oh this boy! He'll be my death.' She pretended to be persecuted by Lester. 'And suppose the flies are only doing their job too? Why mustn't he leave *them* alone?'

'It's his life's work. It's all he knows.'

Lester was very careful of anything that lived, even the smallest insect. He brushed flies away carefully from the donkey's eyes. If there were ants following a grease track across a plate, he shook them gently out of the door, instead of rinsing them under the tap. Once when he and Carrie were digging a bed to plant tomatoes, his spade had cut through a worm, and he had screamed, as if he was the worm, and spent a long time persuading the two ends to join up again.

95

Now he put the spider into his thin brown hand and set it outside the window on the leaf of a creeper. 'Sorry about the web,' he said.

'Talking to a spider! What's to be done with such a boy?' Mrs Figg swept up clouds of dust and blanket fluff from under Michael's bed, and some chocolate papers and apple cores and a dirty cocoa mug as well. 'Go and start a fire under all that rubbish outside, and don't come back in until I call you for lunch.'

At the head of the wide old stairs, which they had once thought were haunted, Carrie paused and looked back to where Lester's mother was bending over the bed, singing to herself, as she tucked in the sheets she had washed. Then she shut her eyes, and with her body full of breath, she felt that she flew down the stairs behind Lester. Did he feel this too? She had never spoken of it, even to him. If she did, she wouldn't be able to – whatever it was she did. It wasn't exactly flying. It was more like – not walking. Not jumping. It was finding yourself at the bottom of the stairs without having touched a step.

By Sunday afternoon, the house at World's End was still shabby, but it was clean.

Em and Carrie had hung the clean bleached curtains on the sparkling windows. Clothes had been washed and put away, and Miss Nuttishall would be able to eat her dinner off the floors, if she so desired.

'You've saved our necks,' Carrie told Mrs Figg.

'They'll have mine if I don't get going. I'm on duty at four.'

It was only then that Carrie discovered that she was a matron in a place called Mount Pleasant, where they put lawless girls who were too young to go to prison.

'I thought you said your mother worked for a secret organization,' she said to Lester.

'Mount Pleasant is an organization. And it's secret. She won't tell me what the girls have done.'

Mrs Figg had brought a beef stew with barley and onions. She put it on to warm before she went home. After she had driven off with Lester, the battered little beetle car bouncing over the pot holes, they realized how comfortable it had been to have her moving so busily about the house, making endless pots of tea, singing old-fashioned songs, calling them for lunch, standing safely at the stove or sink when you came in from outdoors.

Suddenly the kitchen didn't look like a proper kitchen any more. 'I wish Mother was here,' Michael said. He said it again, gloomily, when Tom came home.

'She will be, old chap. You wait.'

'Everyone else has a mother.' Michael was in a misery fit, humped and ruffled like Currier when she went broody. He might be getting flu. That would be all they needed, for Michael to be ill with flu when Miss Nuttishall arrived!

'Some people have fathers,' Em said rather bitterly.

'That's because their stupid fathers haven't got the guts to sail round the world,' Tom said.

'The time he's gone, he could have sailed round the world twice, up and down *and* sideways,' Carrie grumbled.

'I thought you all liked being here on your own.' Tom was in a funny, secret mood. When they asked about their mother, he had only said, 'She's all right,' and he had none of the usual messages from her. Sitting up at the bar, eating Mrs Figg's stew, he was smiling at himself in the decorated mirror. 'I thought that was why you were so afraid of Miss Nuttishall.'

Next morning they made their beds before they went to school, in case she came today.

She did come. When they drove back from school, Tom was at home, which was odd. Had he known she was coming?

As Carrie crossed the yard after feeding John, she saw a strange car in the lane. A dark red saloon. Very clean and square and smug. A Social Working car. The Dreaded Nutshell was here!

She wanted to run and hide, but something made her go into the house, dragging her bare feet. Tom looked hard at them when she came in. 'I left them in the stable,' she mouthed silently. She only had one pair of shoes.

Miss Nuttishall wasn't quite what they had expected. She was fairly young, with a pleated kilt and blue tights. 'What a nice house,' she said politely.

'Yes, isn't it?' Proudly they showed her all over the ground floor, where everything was still beautifully clean and tidy. They hadn't even eaten any breakfast for fear of messing up the kitchen. Let her find fault if she dared!

She dared. 'It's very nice,' she said, 'though it's a bit too clean and tidy for my taste. I think it's better for children to live in a bit of a mess.'

They looked at each other. After all that work!

'Anyway,' went on the Nutshell, not so dreaded now, but terribly, terribly disappointing. 'It doesn't matter. My Department thinks . . . I mean, it's really not the thing for you to live here without your parents. Eh, little fellow?' She put out a hand to tousle Michael's hair, and he ducked away. Tom slipped out of the room, as if he couldn't bear to hear any more.

'So let's discuss ways and means.' Miss Nutshell sat on the chair with the broken springs, going down thump to the floor, but still smiling, because she had made up her mind to be like that. 'Sit down, everybody.' They stayed standing. 'Until your mother comes home, since you really can't stay here alone, let's talk about where you—'

The door opened. In the doorway, pale, thin, groggy but upright, standing by herself, though Tom was close behind, smiling and holding out her hand as if Miss Nuttishall was a welcome guest—

'Mother!' They ran to her, the Dreaded Nutshell forgotten.

That had been Tom's secret last night. He hadn't been to work today. He had been to fetch his mother. She came in the nick of time to save their necks. That was the story of it. In a nutshell.

Twenty

Their mother could not really stand and walk as well as she pretended for Miss Nuttishall. As soon as the Social Worker had driven away – foiled! – in her smug red car, Mother went back upstairs to bed, and there she had to stay most of the time, except when Tom carried her down for supper, or to lie in the hammock that he had made from an old tennis net, strung between two elm trees.

Once long ago when World's End had been Wood's End Inn, with travellers staying here, and a family of boys growing up, before they went off to the war, there had been a tennis court in the corner of the meadow behind the house. That was the flat place where Carrie set up her odd collection of jumps made of what Mr Mismo called 'the fag ends of nothing'.

'If he'll jump those heaps of junk,' he said, 'he'll jump anything. You should take him to a show.'

'Should I?'

His little hat rocked as he threw back his head to laugh, with his scattered teeth showing. 'That five-legged joker? Don't take everything so seriously, old chump.'

One fine spring afternoon, Mother was lying in the hammock, watching Carrie work with John. Lucy the goat went over the jumps behind them. Henry, who had been sheared and felt pounds lighter and years younger, leaped over ahead of them with a flick of his shorn tail.

'Yoo-hoo!' Out of the kitchen door, mincing in a pink skirt too tight and much too short, her hair puffed out in a toppling black beehive, came Aunt Valentina.

Carrie took John quickly behind the corner of the house, but stopped there to listen.

'My dear Alice.' Valentina bent over the hammock to kiss Carrie's mother, although she had never liked her much, because she had once been on the stage and now she did not

99

approve of the way she lived. 'How are you?'

'I'm very well.' She did look much better, her cheeks filling out and colouring, her thick fair hair bouncing again like a bell.

'Well, you don't look it. You're as pale as a blindworm and as thin as a rail and what on earth happened to your hair?' Aunt Val could make you feel terrible even if you were fighting fit.

When Mother began to thank her for helping the children, Valentina said in that crowing voice which could knock ornaments off a shelf, 'It was no more than my duty.'

'Rudolf was kind to give them money . . .'

'We'd have given them more.' It was not her money, but she wasn't going to let him get all the credit. 'But when we offered they were quite rude about it.'

'I'm sorry.' Mother didn't sound as if she believed it.

'Oh well.' Carrie couldn't see, but she could imagine Val tossing her beehive head. 'They needn't feel like beggars any more. While you were in the hospital was one thing, but now that you're home . . .'

Awkward silence. Mother couldn't work yet, but she would never ask for money.

'Let's have some cider,' she said in that light, amused voice which could make something gay even out of being stuck with Valentina on a lovely spring day. 'Carrie!'

She called without raising her voice. She knew Carrie was there, so Carrie came round from the corner of the house.

'No, thanks. I just stopped in to see how you were, and the dear children. Carrie, my pet—' Scream! 'Don't bring that brute too near. What an extraordinary looking horse. Where did you get *that*?'

'I bought him.' Only Lester and Carrie and her mother knew about the horsenapping.

'Oh really?' Valentina's pencilled eyebrows went up into her beehive hair. 'What with?'

You could see the way her mind was working. If *that* was what the children had been doing with the money . . .

'A postcard came for you.' Valentina opened her enormous handbag, for which the world's dwindling population

100

of alligators had been dwindled by one more. Two, if you counted her shoes.

'Who from?' Carrie got off her horse.

'My dear, I don't read other people's postcards,' Valentina said, although the card was crumpled as if she had read it many times and had been carrying it about in the alligator bag for weeks.

'It's from Dad!'

Carrie's shout brought Em out of the back door, 'Why didn't he write to *me*?'

'Yoo-hoo, Esmeralda, what's wrong?' Em had a stocking tied round her head to flatten her curls. 'Have you got a headache?'

'I have now,' Em turned her back on Valentina, and grabbed the postcard.

Carrie had read it quickly. 'He's coming home.' He had drawn

forgetting that Tom was taller than Mother.

'Where from?'

The postmark was rubbed out by Val's thumbs. The picture was called 'Sunset Beach at Harakarawa', but it had been posted months ago. Em took it into the house.

'Oh, Carrie.' Her mother smiled and held out her hand. She didn't say: Why didn't he write to *me*? 'How exciting. He's coming home.'

'And about time.' Valentina did not care to see people too happy. 'About time he came home and took care of his family.'

'He would have.' Mother flared up. She could not sit up in the sagging hammock, so she had to flare up lying down. 'He didn't know what had happened to us.'

'About time he came home to find out. These children – like savages. I was ashamed to sit at table with them. Look at that girl's hair.' Carrie took a piece of it out of her mouth and shook it back. 'Made a proper pigsty of this place, if you ask me. Like some wretched zoo.' She kicked out at Lucy, who had come to sample her shoe buckle, long silky brown ears hanging like a girl's hair.

'I think they've managed wonderfully,' Carrie's mother said. 'I'm proud of them.'

Valentina bent to wipe her shoe with a handkerchief. 'Yes,' she said, 'you would be.'

They were heading into a full-scale fight, and Carrie watched with interest, holding John's reins while he put his head down to eat. If two people you loved had a fight, it made you want to be sick. If someone you loved fought someone you hated, then it was exhilarating – if the one you loved was winning.

But Valentina was winning. She had all the ammunition.

'All right then, if he's such a wonderful husband and father, there's nothing to worry about, is there? Rudolf can certainly use his money for a more worthwhile cause. There are people at the home for the Widows of Disabled Plumbers who will be *very* grateful, I can assure you. And don't forget, my dear Alice,' Valentina said lightly, but her eyes were hard as stones, 'whose house this is, after all. We wouldn't turn you out into the street, I suppose, but there might be a little question of rent . . .'

Mother went pale. She lay in the hammock like a washed-up fish.

'When your sailor man comes rolling home, I'm sure he'll be glad to discuss *that* with his brother Rudolf!'

Having spoiled everyone's day, Valentina felt better. She wanted to see all the children and give them a sixpence.

which was more insulting than giving nothing. She even wanted to see all the animals, probably to report back to Uncle Rudolf that the place was a stinking menagerie.

'A donkey!' she cried when she saw Leonora taking a nap under the twisted old apple tree. 'A little Hee-haw. Oh, memories of my youth! Donkey rides on the beach when I was a little girl . . .'

Centuries ago. Valentina was as old as made no matter, but she flattered herself she looked young for her age. When they lived with her, she used to pretend that people took her and Tom for sister and brother, instead of aunt and nephew. It was disgusting.

'Have a go now,' suggested Michael.

'Should I?' She giggled. 'Oh thrills. It would be just like the gay old times. Put me up someone. Wait – Tom, get my camera out of my bag.' She always had to have pictures taken of herself. 'It will have to be side saddle, my skirt is too tight.'

Michael held Leonora's patient head. Her ears lolled back and forth like furred radar, one forward, one back, which meant she was not sure how she felt.

Valentina bent her leg at the knee. Carrie put both hands under it and gave her a tremendous heave which shot her straight over Leonora's narrow back and into a mud wallow on the other side, just as Tom clicked the camera.

Twenty-one

That was the last they heard of Valentina for some time – except for a bill for cleaning the tight pink skirt.

It was also the last they heard of any money from Uncle Rudolf. 'Who cares?' Mother said. 'Money doesn't matter, after all.'

'Good thing it doesn't,' Em said, 'since we've never had any.'

*She shot straight over Leonora's back just as Tom
clicked the camera*

What little Rainy Day money they had was kept in a china Toby jug on the mantelpiece. Banks made Mother nervous, with their clean spectacled clerks doing complicated sums behind bars. She would never put money in a bank. Carrie still had her teddy bear under the floorboard with the savings tied into the sock, which would one day buy the most beautiful horse in the world.

Meanwhile, she had John. And all the other animals. More and more of them, as the word spread that World's End was a good place to come to.

An old lady, who had to go and live with her daughter, brought her cat in a plastic shopping bag.

'My daughter says I must have Beauty put to sleep.' She was a tiny old lady, looking up at Em with clouded eyes.

'Oh no!' Better to have the daughter put to sleep than that.

Beauty – they changed his name to Brutey – was an old fighter, with half an ear and scars on his head. He chased Julius and Caesar up a tree, where they stayed all day pretending they couldn't get down. But when Em got a ladder, they jumped down on one side of the tree as she climbed up the other.

A bird cage from somewhere. A lovebird that had escaped from a cage and almost died, trying to live wild.

It flew through Tom's window and flopped on the floor, exhausted. Tom made a cage of wire netting, only to keep the cats away. The door was always open and the bird spent most of his time on top of picture frames or riding about in people's hair. He was a male, because he had blue round its beak instead of brown, so they called him Gabriel, nickname Gabby, because when he was stronger he started to talk.

He could call 'Charlie!' and imitate the dog whistle, which was very embarrassing for the dogs. He could do Mr Mismo's: 'Hullo old chump hullo old chump hullo old chump.' You had to throw a towel over the cage to shut him up.

Perpetua had three puppies. Tom, Dick and Harry. Dog Tom, to be different from Boy Tom. They were sand-coloured and sandbag-shaped. When Perpetua was out of the box, Charlie got in and bathed them, like a father taking over the baby when the mother goes shopping.

A boy at school gave Michael a rabbit. Mrs Croker the English teacher gave Carrie a hamster, which her son had got bored with soon after Christmas. The hamster was always soaking wet, because when Perpetua wouldn't let him take care of the puppies, Charlie carried it round in his mouth.

'I've counted up,' Michael said one day. 'Not counting caterpillars and the things that aren't family, there are ninety-six legs in this place.'

Everyone counted in their heads: people, birds, four-legged animals. 'He's right,' Mother said. 'Tell *that* to that woman at the school!'

By 'That woman at the school', she meant Miss McDrane his teacher, whose name she could never remember, but whose visit she would not forget. Miss McDrane had said that Michael was backward, so Mother had informed her that Shakespeare couldn't read until he was fifteen. She made that up, but it shook Miss McDrane.

'Will Shakespeare could spell his own name though.' Miss McDrane probably made that up too. 'That's more than Michael can.'

'Why does he need to,' Mother asked lightly, 'since he knows what it is?'

Miss McDrane had gone away flummoxed. She had come to show Mother the exam papers on which Michael had made designs, but no writing, but Lester had taken her brief-case out of the car and set fire to it, so there was nothing to show.

'Ninety-six? He's wrong you know.' Tom was looking out of the window. 'There are exactly one hundred legs.'

The RSPCA van had come down the lane and stopped by the gate of the yard. Out of it was coming a small Welsh pony, with maps of unknown continents all over his body in black and white.

'His child outgrew him,' the Cruelty Man said, 'and they asked me to find the best home I could.'

'What's his name?' Michael stood with his brown

106

scratched legs apart and his hands on his hips, sizing up the pony. It was just his size.

'Oliver Twist. Because he's always hungry. He always wants more.'

The pony could graze in the meadow. But between John and Leonora and Lucy and Henry and Mr Mismo's cows which kept wandering in through the home-made fence, the turf was getting nibbled bare. Soon they would have to fence off some of the rough grass behind the stable yard. When summer was over, they would have to buy hay. Soon, very soon, said Michael's eager face, alight with love as he stood with an arm thrown over Oliver's back to show *This Is Mine*, soon they must get a saddle and bridle.

So Michael and Carrie went into business. They loaded the wheelbarrow with nicely rotted manure and wheeled it from door to door in the village. No one wanted to buy it. Everyone had chickens, cows, a pony, to fertilize their garden.

Mr Harvey the vet gave them a few shillings for helping Tom at Easter when the boarding kennels were full. But Mr Harvey was almost as poor as they were, because he was always treating animals free. They didn't like to take his money.

'You know what you could do.' He and Tom and Carrie were walking back from the frying shop after work, eating fish and chips in the street. 'You could sell your stuff here on the housing estates. There are no cows or horses here, and these people are mad for a bit of organic fertilizer. Aren't you, Mr Mott?' He called over a garden hedge to a glum old man who was weeding a flower bed.

'What say?' The old man couldn't get up.

'Wouldn't you buy horse manure if you could get it?'

'*Would I?*' The old man's glum face lit up. 'Like gold dust that would be, to my dahlias.'

It was too far to wheel the barrow to the housing estates. Lester knew a man who had an old muck cart for sale cheap.

'Got to spend money to make money,' he said. 'That's the principle of all big business.'

Mother lent them some money out of the china Toby

jug, and Carrie rode John over with his harness on, sitting behind the pad with the long reins coiled round the hames, and brought the muck cart back.

'That nag takes to it like a duck to water.' Mr Mismo shouted rudely from his car as he passed Carrie and Michael going off to the housing estates in the loaded cart, with a shovel sticking up the back like a flag.

'He understands big business!' Carrie shouted as haughtily as it is possible to shout. Mr Mismo's jokes sometimes got boring.

John didn't mind anyway. He liked pulling in harness, and although Carrie drove him without blinkers, he didn't care what came behind.

Michael put a notice on the back of the cart. 'Fine Farm Furtiler. We delver.' They began to make money. When they ran out of horse fertilizer, Mr Mismo let them load up his winter's cow bedding. Soon they had put the cart money back in the Toby jug, and were saving in a willow-pattern vase for Michael's saddle and bridle. They smelled all the time. Em would not sit in the room with them.

Michael rode bareback. Oliver was like a piebald sea horse, with a broad forehead tapering to a delicate square nose and triangular pricked-up ears. After a while, he didn't buck Michael off any more, so Michael took him to the village fête and offered pony rides at sixpence a go.

Oliver hated it. Small girls with pinching fingers clambered on and off his back, sometimes two at once, sometimes facing backwards. Michael clung on to his halter rope while his blue Welsh pony eye rolled and his little ears flicked back and forth.

'Make him go!' the little girls yelled. 'I want to gallop!' But when Michael clicked his tongue and trotted with Oliver and the girls began to jiggle and jounce, they yelled, 'I want to get down!'

One of them smeared candy floss on the pony's neck, and the flies swarmed. Oliver swished his thick tail and shivered his skin, but he could only scratch by reaching forward with his back hoof. When he did that, a child yelled, 'He tried to kick me!'

Oliver was furious. Michael was red and puffing. He had only made two-and-six, because most of the girls ran off without paying. When he went to get a lemonade, a large rough boy untied Oliver's rope, climbed on his back, whacked him with a stick and got bucked off into the bran tub full of Lucky Dips.

The Lucky Dip lady was decent about it. The boy was not.

'I'll sue you for having a dangerous beast!' he shouted, brushing bran off his bottom. 'I'll have him shot!'

Michael began to cry, burying his face in Oliver's black and white mane.

'Unless you give me all the money you made.'

Michael handed over the two-and-six and took Oliver home.

'That wasn't fair,' Carrie said, when Michael told her the story.

'No. Those girls cheated, and that boy was bigger than me.'

'I mean, it wasn't fair to give rides on Oliver.'

'I wanted money.'

'Money doesn't matter,' Carrie said. 'Not as much as your pony.'

But then something happened which made it seem different. 'Money doesn't matter,' Mother said. But when something like this happened, it did – oh, it did.

Twenty-two

Some miles away from World's End, away from the woods and the curly stream and the gentle hills, a large town sprawled on a flat plain, spreading ugliness as it grew.

Carrie had only been there once, at Christmas, to see the lights. The lights were all right, but the town was horrible, noisy and smelly and full of worried people whose faces didn't look a bit like Christmas.

But Lester's mother had been given two concert tickets by a woman who came to play the flute to the lawless girls at Mount Pleasant. 'Time you two listened to something but your own daft notions,' Mrs Figg said, so Carrie and Lester went into town one afternoon on a bus.

The concert was in a big theatre. Lester and Carrie sat at the front of the highest balcony, from where they could have flown on to the stage if it had not been a bristling forest of violin bows, sawing up and down.

While the orchestra was tuning up, with music like howling cats, they ate biscuits and dropped crumbs on the heads of people sitting below. They tore pages out of their programmes to see how long they would take to flutter down.

'What a cheek, letting kids come here alone,' a woman grumbled.

'It's a scientific experiment,' Lester explained. 'How do you think the Law of Gravity was discovered, Madam?'

He could be very polite when he liked, but the woman only said, 'What a cheek,' and snorted like a horse.

When the music started, Lester leaned forward and watched the arms of the conductor, and the hands of the pianist, and the fingers of the fiddlers, and the cheeks of the trumpeters, and the legs of the man who made the bass drum pound with his right foot and the cymbals clash with his left. Carrie leaned back with her eyes closed and listened to the colours and images and wild throbbing dreams that the music poured into her head.

She had never heard music like that before. Afterwards, she reeled out into the street like a drunk man. Lester pranced beside her, singing special bits of the music, and conducting the air. People turned to stare at them.

'Don't let's go home.' They were supposed to go straight to the bus, but all of a sudden this crowded Saturday town was an adventure. The roar of traffic and feet and voices made a wild music that led them on from street to street, weaving between the busy legs, dashing across at corners under the snub noses of panting buses, stopping to stare into lighted windows, exploring archways and dark alleys.

'Follow me.' Lester spun ahead and ducked into a narrow opening between two tall buildings. Carrie thought she had lost him. She ran down the narrow street, searching everywhere. Was it true then, that he could fly? She looked up at the slate roofs and chimney pots. She looked down behind dustbins and parked cars and into the doorways of the dusty little shops in this deserted street.

A pet shop. She stopped dead in front of a small dirty window, low down, because the shop was half below pavement level. On a sawdust floor, three fat puppies played and a nest of kittens slept, and a large sad dog with hanging ears lay with its eyes open, watching the street. Over the partition between the window and the shop, a grinning face suddenly appeared. A monkey? Lester. Carrie let out her breath and went down the steps into the shop.

What could one do about such a place as this? Although the puppies were happy, because they were young and foolish, it was a sad place, where all kinds of animals that were not meant to be pets quietly despaired.

A Mexican coatimundi, its heavy striped tail sweeping the cage floor, its long rubbery nose endlessly questing for freedom. A limp ferret like the collar of Valentina's Spring coat. Tropical birds huddled close together on a perch for comfort or warmth. A mournful snake. A tank of baby green turtles, caught by the thousand in some warm Southern swamp. They climbed hopelessly over one another, blindly wanting a way out; but if one got out by being bought, it might not even live for as long as it took for a child to get sick of it.

Mice, fish, canaries, hamsters, the long-eared dog who watched the street. If you couldn't buy them all, what could you do about them? What could you do about the sulking parrot? What could you do about the little black woolly monkey who wore a collar and chain and sat with its back turned, shivering, on top of its cage?

'You want to buy something?' The owner of the shop was a pale underground man with white flesh and soft pudgy hands. Not a Black Bernie sort of villain. The animals

111

looked fed and fairly clean. But they were sad.

'Just looking round,' Lester said airily, standing on his toes to keep the top of the situation.

'You young devils. I'm sick of it.' The man sat on a stool behind the counter and read his evening paper.

The little monkey on the chain had a blunt black face with thick woolly hair and big dark eyes like wet chocolate. When Carrie talked softly to him, he looked round over his shoulder, then turned away and swung his head from side to side, sorrowing for his lost jungle.

'He's shivering,' Carrie said. 'He's cold.'

'Cold my eye,' said the man, who was wearing a thick jersey. 'He's nervous, the silly beggar.'

'What of?'

'You, of course. How would you like to have some cheeky young devil poke his face into yours and jabber, jabber, jabber?'

But it was not Carrie who made the monkey nervous. When the man stood up and shook his newspaper and said, 'Buzz off!' the monkey cringed at his voice.

'It's all right, little monkey.' Carrie put out her hand, but he was watching the man. She went to the counter. 'How—' Her voice came out in an anxious squeak. 'How much is the monkey?'

The man had sat down again with his newspaper. 'Ten pounds,' he said without looking up. 'Now buzz off, I said. I'm busy.'

As they went to the door, the little black monkey turned round. He stared at Carrie, his dark eyes seeking something she could not give, then pushed his lips forward into a nervous, coaxing smile.

'Come on,' Lester said, as if he couldn't bear it either.

In the street, Carrie turned to him in distress, 'He looked at me. Oh, did you see? He looked at me.'

'Can't do much about it really,' the Cruelty Man said. He had stopped in at World's End to see Leonora and Oliver Twist. 'That chap treats the animals fairly well, though I'll have to go to his shop if this cold spell goes on, and see about the temperature. We do inspect all the pet shops, you know, but we can't close them all up, even if we'd like to.'

'But that monkey ...' Carrie had it on the brain. She could not get it out of her head, the dark seeking eyes and the anxious smile. 'What will happen to him?'

'Someone will buy him, I suppose.'

'I wish I could.'

'So do I, my dear.' The Cruelty Man had a wise, kind face and blue eyes that crinkled almost shut when he smiled. 'You'd take care of it properly. Animals like that, they get bought on a fanciful whim by someone who wants to go one better than the neighbours. Then when they find it's not just a more comical cat or dog, they're flabbergasted. They don't know what to do with it.'

'So what do they do?'

'They try and sell it back to the shop or give it to a zoo, if it's not already too ill. Importing monkeys and things for pets is all wrong. There's a stop being put to it.'

Too late for poor little Loonie. That was the insulting name the pet shop man had given to the monkey.

When Mrs Figg had to go down to take one of her lawless girls to see the magistrate, Carrie went with her. The girl's name was Liza. She was friendlier than most lawless girls of that age. In the car, she told Carrie what life was like at Mount Pleasant. Mount Putrid, she called it, and held her nose.

'You girls are all the same,' Mrs Figg said amiably. 'Grumble, grumble.'

Carrie told Liza about the monkey. 'He looked at me,' she said, and Liza said, 'If I had more than just what I stand up in, I'd buy him for you.'

Nobody had any money. When Carrie went down into the pet shop, the man was making his tea in the back, and Loonie clung to Carrie, loving her, patting her with his delicate hands, pushing at her lips with his long skinny fingers to make her go on talking.

'You again?' The pale man came through with a steaming mug.

'I just came back to see the monkey.' He clung to her like

a baby. 'If he were mine, I'd call him Joey.'

'Yes,' said the man rudely, 'you would.'

'I came back to ask how much?'

'I told you. Ten pounds.' He was crosser than last time.

'If I could *get* ten pounds,' Carrie said, 'would you let me take him?'

'Might.' The man sucked at his hot tea. 'Might not. Depend if he was still here. There's a chap interested in him for his business. He's got this old barrel organ, see, and he goes round the streets. You don't see barrel organs much any more. Bit of a curiosity. Specially with a little monkey like this dressed up in a red coat, holding out the hat for pennies.'

Carrie laid her cheek on the monkey's woolly head. 'I don't think he'd like that,' she said.

'Oh, get out.' The man was even crosser. 'You get on my nerves, you honestly do.'

When Carrie said goodbye to the monkey, she whispered into his ear, 'I'll come back.'

Would he still be here? Would she find his cage empty and have to walk through the town listening for hurdy-gurdy music, until she found him shivering in a silly red coat, chained to the top of the barrel organ?

Waiting at a corner for Mrs Figg and Liza, Carrie read a poster advertising a local horse show.

'Valuable Prizes,' it said. 'Special Junior Jumping. First Prize £10.'

Everybody told Carrie not to take John to the horse show.

'It's too much to ask of him,' her mother said. 'Why make him compete? Why can't he just be a horse?'

'He's got to be the best horse.'

'Those jumps will be murder,' Mr Mismo said. 'They'll start at four feet.'

'He can do that. You've seen him.'

'He – well look, Carrie,' Tom said. 'He won't look like the other show jumpers.'

'That doesn't matter. Jumping isn't judged on con-formation.'

114

'What on earth will you wear?' Em asked. 'They won't even let you *in* without a jockey cap.'

'I'll borrow one when I get there.'

'When I took Oliver Twist to the village fête,' Michael said to no one in particular, 'Carrie said it wasn't fair. What's the difference?'

'John's getting stale,' Mother said, watching from a seat on the fallen tree while Carrie went over and over and over the wall she had made out of two old doors, until John finally got fed up and ran out.

'He's got to learn.' Carrie came back to her, flushed and angry. 'He doesn't know enough.'

'Enough for what?'

'To win.'

'Oh, Carrie, why must he? Why must you suddenly beat everyone?'

'I need the prize money.'

'What for?'

'Something special.' Carrie had not told anyone about the monkey. If she wasn't able to save him, she wouldn't want their pity.

'Can't you save for it?'

'There's no *time*! Oh!' She yanked John crossly round. 'It's hateful never to have any money!'

She set her jaw and went at the wall again. Her mother got up and went into the house.

A day or two later, when Em took in her tea before she went to school, Mother's bed was neatly made. Her night-dress was hanging behind the door. Her blue dress and sandals were gone. So was she.

They found a note propped against the bread crock. She had gone to work in the kitchen at Mount Pleasant.

She came back that evening with Mrs Figg. She could hardly get out of the little car, hardly walk up the path.

'You should all be ashamed,' Mrs Figg said when she had put Mother to bed and come downstairs where the four of them waited, silent and afraid. 'Letting your mother go to work when she's still so weak. If I'd known she was in the kitchen, I'd have put a stop to it, but the first I knew was a great hullabaloo and one of the girls came running down the corridor screaming, "The new cook has fainted!" '

'Oh – poor Mother!'

'Poor silly Mother,' Mrs Figg said. 'Why on earth did she go and do a daft thing like that?'

No one said anything. Only Carrie knew.

Twenty-three

Everything was going wrong. The doctor said Mother had to stay in bed again. She could not even go out to the hammock.

Everyone except Carrie was still against the horse show, including John. He wasn't working well. He was bored and careless over the familiar jumps. He rubbed his tail until there was a bare bristly patch at the top. He lost a shoe the day before the show when there was no time to go over the hill to the blacksmith. It was only a hind shoe. Carrie would have to risk it.

His mane was a disaster, uneven, but too straggly to pull, and half over on the wrong side from having his head down to graze. Carrie spent two hours trying to plait it, but it stood up at odd angles in wispy knots. Two of them came undone as she started off for the show very early in the morning. To crown it all, John pretended to be slightly lame. He sometimes did that when he started out, an old trick remembered from the days when he didn't like his work. But why today?

Jogging along through the chill grey morning, Carrie imagined herself on her dream horse. He would be a thoroughbred, bright bay with two white feet and a star like a clean snowflake. She would be in a black jacket with a white stock and yellow breeches, and a jockey cap with her name on the purple silk lining. You could see your face in her boots. As she rode into the show grounds on her splendid horse, people would stare and exclaim, and other competitors would grit their teeth.

'What horse is *that*?' The sixteen junior riders were in the collecting ring while the jumps were put up. Carrie stood next to a girl with no chin and a big bottom on a magnificent black horse who had tried to bite her as she hauled herself into the saddle.

'Don John.' That was John's show name, from one of the poems Mrs Croker recited:

> *Strong gongs groaning as the guns boom far,*
> *Don John of Austria is going to the war.*

'Who's riding it?'

'I am.' Carrie wanted to look at the jumps not talk.

'Like that?'

Carrie was wearing jeans and Wellingtons, a white shirt of Tom's. 'I got too hot.' (It was raining.) 'I took off my jacket.'

'Where's your cap?'

'I lost it. I was going to ask you. Your number's before mine. After you've jumped, could I borrow yours?'

'Sorry.' The girl moved her horse away.

Carrie didn't like to ask anyone else. They all seemed to know each other and were chattering without listening, telling tall stories about what their horses had won or were going to win. All the horses were very grand.

She stood alone by the side of the ring, John perfectly relaxed, except for trying to get his head down to eat grass. Grass, at a time like this! When Carrie saw some of the riders looking at him and sniggering, she looked behind her to show she thought they were laughing at something else.

Mr Mismo was behind her, wearing his best green felt cap low down, to look knowledgeable, his large bulk overlapping a shooting stick. 'Doesn't look so bad for a muck cart horse,' he said.

Carrie bit her lip. She couldn't take that kind of joke today.

117

'Keep your pecker up, old chump.'

She gave him a sick smile. She had ordered her family to keep away from her, but she was glad to see Mr Mismo, jokes and all.

'Now look, I'll tell you what you do.' He had lent her the entry money, so was bossier than ever. 'You start him out slow, see. That brush is nothing. The gate's tricky, and watch that corner. You ease him up, then two strides before your in-and-out, push him on . . .'

Carrie couldn't listen. Her eyes were on the jumping ring, where the judge and stewards were at the last fence, the triple bar, with their measuring stick.

The ring steward put the hunting horn to his lips. The thin thrilling sound made all the horses lift their heads and prick their ears, even John who had never gone hunting. Or had he? Had he ever been to a show before? His past was a mystery. The gate opened, and the first horse trotted into the ring, a girl like an ape on a bay thoroughbred with the two white feet and a star. Carrie's dream horse. Oh well, of course, it would win. Better not look. She had to look.

The bay thoroughbred put his ears back even while the ape girl put him into his circling canter. He stopped at the brush. She whacked. He hopped over with his head in the air. He got stickily halfway round the jumps, and refused three times at the high gate. The girl whacked him and rode out with a face of fury.

'One down,' Mr Mismo said, leaning on the rail of the ring and sucking his pipe as calmly as if he were at a cattle show. 'Fifteen to go.'

Nobody did well. The jumps were big and spaced in a difficult way. Every horse made some mistake. There were no clear rounds. Carrie began to feel a little less sick. Perhaps . . .? She watched a boy on a big chestnut crash all the bricks out of the top of the wall, and a good looking grey dump his girl in the middle of the in-and-out.

The steward blew the horn to show that she was disqualified for falling off, and the girl limped out after the grey, which had already headed for the gate.

Suddenly it was Carrie's turn. 'Number fifty-two – Caroline Fielding on Don John.'

'Where's your cap?' The man at the gate called to her.

'I lost it.'

'Lend her one, someone. Come on, you're wasting time.'

Someone handed her a cap. It was too big. Even as she cantered round in her approach circle, it came down over her eyes and she had to take a hand off the reins and push it back. Someone in the crowd said, 'Coo, look at this one!' John leaped easily over the brush fence. 'Never knew mules could jump,' someone else said, and there was laughter.

The laughter stopped as he took the high rustic fence, his straggly plaits and the familiar view of the back of his wide ears rising before Carrie like an antelope. There was a roaring in her ears that was the roar of wind and hooves, the roar of the crowd, the roar of glory. Jump after jump came up, he hammered the turf, rose, soared, landed – he could not make a mistake!

We're going to win, Carrie thought numbly. She clung. She wasn't riding. She was hanging on, with her legs weak and her breath gasping.

Down the middle to the last fence, the triple bar, John took off confidently, standing far back. Carrie was left behind. Her hands flew up, she jerked him in the mouth, and he crashed through the rails as she fell off.

'All right?' Someone ran over to her. She pushed him away and got up blindly, the cap over her eyes. John was standing by her, eating grass.

'You could have won.' She pushed back the cap and put her face into his neck.

I don't care, she thought he said.

The horn blew, quite merrily. Carrie walked out of the ring, not holding the reins. John followed her with all his plaits undone.

He could have won. I wasn't good enough.

When she was half asleep, jumping into a dream, Penny-Come-Quick was at the window without being called. She knew the tread of his impatient feet on the still night air.

Jump after jump came up — he could not make a mistake

She went to the window. It was not Penny, arching his grey silk neck to the call of the stars. It was not a dream horse. It was John.

And she knew every line of him, every glance of his honest eye, the plain set of his big ears, the warmth of his breath in her hand, and she knew that he was all she wanted.

They galloped to the star, and a small crowd gathered round to hear about the show.

'He could have won,' Carrie said, 'but I wasn't good enough.' It was easy to be honest up here.

'Isn't it always the way?' said Marocco. In the days of Queen Elizabeth, he had been a famous dancing horse, whose tricks were so clever that the people of those days called it black magic. 'Almost any horse could jump, if it wasn't for the clumsy clots on top.'

'All horses can jump five feet,' said a fat Shetland who didn't look as though he could jump five inches.

'Why don't they jump out of a paddock then?' Carrie asked.

'Because they are too stupid.' Marocco winked. He was one of the cleverest horses on the star.

'No,' John said, 'it's because they know when they're well off.'

Twenty-four

The next day was Sunday. How live through it until Monday when the pet shop would be open?

Carrie had unpinned the teddy bear and taken out the sock and counted the money once more. A few notes, and the rest of it in silver and pennies. It came to nine pounds fifteen shillings.

'Will you lend me five shillings?' she asked her mother.

'I will.' Mother was still very tired and weak. It hurt her to sit up, so she lay on her bag in the sagging, uncomfortable bed and watched John and Oliver, and Leonora and Henry and Lucy and Perpetua's older son, Moses moving peacefully about the slope of the meadow. She and Em played draughts with bottle caps on a piece of chequered linoleum. Michael read stories to her. She was the only person who could properly understand a story when Michael read it.

He was reading her an old book called *Gamble Gold*, which he had found in the attic. He read:

'Budge shake his ear and Gammly God took up his poston and thew his first piece of sat . . sate . . . slate. It truck the water and gave one long lap, then a constant run for little laps, and truck the possite bank, and then a wonfull thing happended, of it come back cross the water again on the redound. Bug braking furishly all the time until it landed to Gammly foot.'

'Gamble,' Carrie said. 'Gamble Gold.'

' "Thirty-eight," said Gammly God . . .'

Carrie went down to get the five shillings from the Toby jug on the mantelpiece.

She was so happy today that even hearing a horn and 'Yoo-hoo!' could not spoil it. She greeted Valentina with a smile, but her aunt marched into the house, demanding, 'Where's your mother?'

'Upstairs in bed. She's not well.'

'I knew it was too soon to leave the hospital.'

'Not well enough to see anyone.' Carrie tried to get between Valentina and the staircase, but she pushed past and went up into Mother's room, stamping the knotted old boards with her hard heels.

Carrie followed. 'Well, he did come,' she was saying. 'Your precious husband Jerome arrived at dawn – he would, so dramatic – and woke us up.'

'Jerry?' Mother couldn't sit up, but her tired eyes sparkled and her mouth curved into a glad smile. 'Where is he?'

'Search me. He'd been to your old house and found the blackened ruin. He came to us, in a high old state, so I told him what I thought of him going off into the blue with no thought for his duty to his family. He told me to mind my own business – he's just as rude as ever – and when I said, "I bet you have no idea where your precious family are," he wasn't going to admit it. He said, "Of course I have," and banged out. He broke a pane of glass in the front door. That will cost—'

'But he *doesn't* know!' Mother's face had fallen from brightness.

'Who doesn't?'

Carrie and Michael jumped round, and then ran to the door. Mother, who couldn't sit up, sat up and held out her arms. Valentina looked as if she'd seen a ghost.

'See, Val, I told you I knew.' With Em clutching behind, and Carrie and Michael hanging on him like weights, their father came and knelt beside the bed. 'What's wrong?'

'I broke my back,' said Mother with a broad grin.

'My God – how?'

'Trying to save someone's life,' Carrie said.

'And did you?'

'Yes. It was mine.' Michael pushed his face up under his arm. 'Laddy Ace. What does that mean?'

His father was wearing a bright blue jersey with *Lady Alice* across the chest.

'It's the name of my new boat. Well – I haven't got her yet, but the jersey is a start.'

'Where's the other boat?'

'It sank.'

He wore a pair of red bell-bottom trousers and rope sandals. He had grown a thick black beard. He looked like a pirate.

When Valentina had stamped away, he laughed and told them he had guessed she would come to them, so he waited till she came out, then got a taxi and followed her car.

'Oh, by the way.' He scratched his black curly head. 'Anyone got any money? The driver's waiting.'

'No, he's not.' Tom had met Valentina in the lane, heard the news and raced upstairs. 'Aunt Val was so furious, she backed her car into the taxi and the driver got nasty, so to shut him up, she paid his fare.'

Twenty-five

Carrie had not seen Lester since she had caught sight of him at the horse show, perched in a tree like a rook, but as she walked through the beechwood to the crossroads where the bus stopped, he came casually out from the tall grey trees and fell into step beside her.

'Why aren't you at school?' she asked.

'I'm fed up with the school lark, so I came to see if you were too.'

'I'm going into town to buy that monkey.' Carrie showed him the sock with the money knotted into the toe.

'Your horse money?'

'I don't need it for that now.'

Lester nodded. He was as good as a dog for quick understanding.

From the bus station in town, they ran to the pet shop, ducking and swerving among the slow Monday morning people. The owner was sitting with his elbows on the counter, eating a plate of greasy bacon.

'Where's the monkey?' Carrie's eyes had flown at once to Joey's cage.

'What monkey?' He behaved as if he had never seen Carrie before.

'You know, the one I liked. The one you said cost ten pounds.

'I got thirteen pound ten for him, so that shows how much *you* know.' His jaw worked on the bacon. There was grease round his pale mouth.

'You mean, you sold him?'

'I'm not in business for my health, you know.'

'If you are, it's a failure,' Lester murmured standing by the snake's tank, trying to hypnotize it with his eye.

'You mean—' Carrie couldn't believe it. She had not thought of this – 'you mean, you sold him to the organ grinder?' Into her mind jumped a vision of Joey in a little red jacket, shivering on top of a painted hurdy gurdy, while jaded Monday people hurried past paying no attention to his outstretched cap.

The vision pushed tears forward, but the man said stupidly, 'What organ grinder? A lady came into this shop a few days ago, and nothing would satisfy her but she'd take that monkey with her, sitting up in the back of a big car like Lord Muck himself.'

'I know his cousin, the Marquess of Mud—' Lester began, but Carrie said quickly, 'Please tell me the lady's name.'

'Let's see.' The man pretended to look through a long sales list in a notebook, running his soft white finger down the page, though Carrie could see, reading upside down, that it was a laundry list. 'Name of Horrobin,' he said, 'because she's horribly rich, ha, ha.'

Instead of spoiling his digestion, the greasy bacon seemed to improve his mood. 'Lives in that swanky block of flats in the Broadway. Fairview Court, they call it, because there's no tennis court and no view.'

'Could we go and see her?'

'I doubt you two will get past the porter.' The man looked them up and down, as if they were a joke too.

Mrs Horrobin lived in the penthouse flat on top of the tall new block of flats known as Fairview Court. She was, as the man had said, horribly rich. Lester and Carrie, shown in by a butler on to a thick white carpet in their faded shorts and grubby gym shoes, found her on a satin sofa, wearing a long ruffled gown with ostrich feathers at neck and hem, and smoking gold-tipped cigarettes. The little monkey was in a cage in the corner of the luxurious room. He was wearing frilly knickers and a silly baby's dress with blue ribbons.

'My dear children, I'm so glad you came.' Mrs Horrobin wasn't as horrible as they had feared. 'No one has been near me since I bought that dreadful Louise.'

'He's not a girl. I call him Joey,' Carrie said. 'Why did you buy him?'

'She was so *sweet*.' Mrs Horrobin was one of those people who never bother to get the sex of an animal right.

125

'And I thought she would go with my new linen suit. Just the same shade. But oh, what a stupid girl I was!' She was at least fifty, and showed every day of it. 'Yesterday, I was playing with her, and she bit me.' She held up a finger with an enormous bandage on it. 'I may die of blood poisoning any minute. Look out, she's savage!'

Carrie was opening the door of the cage. She picked up the monkey and held him close, cuddling him. He had chewed most of the blue ribbons off his dress and put his foot through the hem. He chattered and clucked in a soft pleased way, then sat on her shoulder and began to pick over her long sandy hair as if she were another monkey.

'Why was she so mean to me and not to you?' complained Mrs Horrobin.

'He wasn't mean,' Carrie said. 'He's a boy, not a girl, and boy monkeys have to practise being top dog, so they can work their way up in the group. If you'd been his mother, you'd have been pleased that he was being so manly.'

'Do I look like her mother?' Mrs Horrobin picked up a mirror from a little table by a sofa and stared in horror at her painted, pouting face. She lit another cigarette, set fire to a bit of the ostrich feather and patted it out, coughing. 'That beastly Louise doesn't know her luck, being bought by me. She's an ungrateful, savage brute.'

'You can't change an animal's instincts by making it live with people,' Lester explained patiently. This was so obvious to him and Carrie, it was surprising that a grown-up had to have it explained. 'Every wild animal has to fight for his place in the herd.'

'This isn't a herd.' Mrs Horrobin coughed through a cloud of tobacco smoke. 'This is sixty-seven Fairview Court. So she'd better make up her mind, either she's a pet or she isn't, because I'm going to give her to the University laboratory for research.'

'Oh no!' Carrie said. 'If you don't want him, sell him to me. I've got the money. Not quite what you paid for him, but he's secondhand now, so—'

'I've already rung up the University.' Mrs Horrobin lit another cigarette from the gold stub of the last. 'That useless

126

creature may as well do her bit for medical science.'

Lester came close to her, walking without weight on the white carpet in his grey tattered gym shoes. 'Did you know,' he said softly, 'that they make them smoke cigarettes—'

'I think that's dogs.' Carrie liked to get facts right, but Lester kicked her on the ankle.

'Did you know that they make them smoke a packet a day to see how dangerous it is for people?'

'That's what I told you.' Mrs Horrobin would not look him in the eye. 'It's for medical science.'

'And did you know,' Lester went on, 'that they make them smoke and smoke until their lungs are like lumps of coal?'

Mrs Horrobin hastily put out her cigarette. 'Oh, you children.' She was irritable now, wanting a cigarette and yet not wanting to smoke one. 'Oh, take the beastly animal and leave me alone!'

'How much?' Carrie was holding Joey with one hand and trying to undo the knot of the sock with the other.

'I'll *give* her away,' Mrs Horrobin said, 'to get rid of the three of you.'

They went down in the lift, with the monkey clinging to Carrie like a drowning man, and sauntered casually out into the street, as if a monkey round your neck was the latest fashion wear.

Carrie was swinging the sock full of money.

'What are you going to do with it?' Lester asked. 'Put it back under the floorboard?'

They were passing a furniture shop as he spoke. For answer, Carrie turned into the shop and bought a new mattress for her mother's bed.

'How are you going to get it home?' The assistant was a pleasant young man, who had not minded Lester and Carrie and Joey trying all the beds by lying down and bouncing on them.

'On the bus.'

'The conductress will love you. A monkey *and* a mattress . . .'

127

'I'll drive in and fetch it.' Carrie was still lying on the mattress she had chosen, with Joey curled between her head and shoulder. Lester reclined on a double bed like Mrs Horrobin, smoking an imaginary cigarette.

'Girls fool me.' The assistant scratched his head. 'You can't be old enough to drive a car?'

'A horse and trap.'

'In this traffic? Bit scary for a horse.'

'My horse John will go anywhere.'

'Then don't ask him to come into this stinking town.' The assistant smiled down at her. 'We'll be glad to deliver – free of charge. Where is it to?'

'World's End.' Into Carrie's mind came a picture of the old stone inn, with Michael's painted sign swinging gently over the door, the curving tile roof, a banner of smoke rising from the kitchen chimney, the meadow dotted with animals. Mother in the bed under the window with the breeze blowing the faded curtains, Dad on the floor with his pirate beard, telling her tall tales of the sea.

'That's where we live.' She lay on the new mattress with her hands behind her head and the little monkey falling asleep in her hair. 'World's End.'